I0550088

The Gray Madam & Other Stories by Anna Katharine Green

Anna Katharine Green was born in Brooklyn, New York on November 11th, 1846.

Anna's initial ambition was to be a poet. However that path failed to ignite any significant interest and she turned to fiction writing. She published her first—and most famous work in 1878—'The Leavenworth Case'. Wilkie Collins praised it and it sold extremely well.

It led to Anna writing 40 novels and to becoming known as 'the mother of the detective novel.'

In helping to shape the genre she brought many other innovations including a series detective: her main character was detective Ebenezer Gryce of the New York Metropolitan Police Force, but in three novels he is assisted by the nosy society spinster Amelia Butterworth, another innovation and a prototype for Miss Marple, Miss Silver and others.

She also invented the 'girl detective': in the character of Violet Strange, a debutante with a secret life as a sleuth. Anna's other innovations included the now familiar dead bodies in libraries, newspaper clippings as "clews," the coroner's inquest, and expert witnesses. Yale Law School once used her books to demonstrate how damaging it can be to rely on circumstantial evidence.

Her career was now well advanced and she was much admired.

On November 25, 1884, Green married the actor and stove designer, and later noted furniture maker, Charles Rohlfs, who was seven years her junior. They had three children; Rosamund, Roland and Sterling.

Although Anna was a progressive she did not approve of many of her feminist contemporaries, and was opposed to women's suffrage.

On November 25, 1884, Anna married the actor and noted furniture maker, Charles Rohlfs, who was seven years her junior. They had three children; Rosamund, Roland and Sterling.

Anna Katharine Green died on April 11, 1935 in Buffalo, New York, at the age of 88.

Index of Contents
THE GRAY MADAM
MIDNIGHT IN BEAUCHAMP ROW
AS TOLD BY MR. GRYCE
THE DOCTOR, HIS WIFE, AND THE CLOCK
X. Y. Z. A DETECTIVE STORY
CHAPTER I – The Mysterious Rendezvous
CHAPTER II – The Black Domino
CHAPTER III - An Unexpected Calamity
CHAPTER IV – In the Library
CHAPTER V - The Yellow Domino
THREE THOUSAND DOLLARS

THE GRAY MADAM

Was it a specter?

For days I could not answer this question. I am no believer in spiritual manifestations, yet—But let me tell my story.

I was lodging with my wife on the first floor of a house in Twenty-seventh street. I had taken the apartments for three months, and we had already lived in them two and found them sufficiently comfortable. The back room we used as a bedroom, and while it communicated with the hall, we invariably made use of the front parlor-door to go in and out of. Two great leaves of old mahogany connected the two rooms, and as we received but few friends, these doors usually stood half open.

One morning, my wife being ill, I left her lying in bed and stepped into the parlor preparatory to going out for breakfast. It was late—nine o'clock, probably—and I was hastening to leave, when I heard a sound behind me—or did I merely feel a presence?—and, turning, saw a strange and totally unknown woman coming toward me from my wife's room.

As I had just left that room, and as there was no way of getting into it except through a door we always kept locked, I was so overpowered by my astonishment that I never thought of speaking or moving until she had passed me. Then I found voice, and calling out "Madam!" endeavored to stop her.

But the madam, if madam she was, passed on as quietly, as mechanically even, as if I had not raised my voice, and, before I could grasp the fact that she was melting from before me, flitted through the hall to the front door and so out, leaving behind on the palm of my hand the "feel" of her wool dress, which I had just managed to touch.

Not understanding her or myself or the strange thrill awakened by this contact, I tore open the front door and looked out, expecting, of course, to see her on the steps or on the sidewalk in front. But there was no one of her appearance visible, and I came back questioning whether I was the victim of a hallucination or just an everyday fool. To satisfy myself on this important question I looked about for the hall-boy, with the intention of asking him if he had seen any such person go out, but that young and inconsequent scamp was missing from his post as usual, and there was no one within sight to appeal to.

There was nothing to do but to re-enter my rooms, where my attention was immediately arrested by the sight of my wife sitting up in bed and surveying me with a look of unmistakable astonishment.

"Who was that woman?" she asked. "And how came she in here?"

So she had seen her too.

"What woman, Lydia? I have not let in any woman. Did you think there was a woman in this room?"

"Not in that room," she answered hoarsely, "but in this one. I saw her just now passing through the folding doors. Wilbur, I am frightened. See how my hands shake. Do you think I am sick enough to imagine things?"

I knew she was not, but I did not say so. I thought it would be better for her to think herself under some such delusion.

"You were dozing," said I. "If you had seen a woman here, you could tell me how she looked."

"And I can," my wife broke in excitedly. "She was like the ghosts we read of, only that her dress and the veil or drapery she wore were all gray. Didn't you see her? You must have seen her. She went right by you—a gray woman, all gray; a lady, Wilbur, and slightly lame. Could I have dreamed all that?"

"You must have!" I cried, shaking the one door communicating with the hall, so she might see it was locked, and even showing her the key of it, lying in its accustomed place behind the bureau cushion. Yet I was in no satisfied condition myself, for she had described with the greatest accuracy the very person I had myself seen. Had we been alike the victims of a spiritual manifestation?

This was Tuesday. On Friday my question seemed to receive an answer. I had been down town, as usual, and on returning found a crowd assembled in front of my lodging-house. A woman had been run over and was being carried into our rooms. In the glimpse I caught of her I saw that she was middle-aged and was wrapped in a long black cloak. Later, this cloak fell off, as her hat had done long before, and I perceived that her dress was black and decent.

She was laid on our bed and every attention paid her. But she had been grievously injured about the head and gradually but surely sank before our eyes. Suddenly she roused and gave a look about her. It was a remarkable one—a look of recognition and almost of delight. Then she raised one hand and, pointing with a significant gesture into the empty space before her, sank back and died.

It was a sudden ending, and, anxious to see its effect upon my wife, who was standing on the other side of the bed, I glanced her way with some misgiving. She showed more feeling than I had anticipated. Indeed her countenance was a study, and when, under, the influence of my scrutiny she glanced my way, I saw that something of deeper import than this unexpected death in our rooms lay at the bottom of her uneasy look.

What that was, I was soon to know, for catching up from amid the folds of the woman's gray-lined cloak a long gray veil which had fallen at the bedside, she disposed it softly about the woman's face, darting me a look full of significance.

"You remember the vision I had the morning when I was sick?" she whispered softly in my ear.

I nodded, secretly thrilled to my very heart's core.

"Well, it was a vision of this woman. If she were living and on her feet and wrapped, as I have shown you, in this veil, you would behold a living picture of the person I saw passing out of this room that morning."

"I shall not dispute you," I answered. Alas, I had myself perceived the likeness the minute the veil had fallen about the pinched but handsome features!

"A forewarning," whispered my wife, "a forewarning of what has this day happened under our roof. It was a wraith we saw. Wilbur, I shall not spend another night in these rooms."

And we did not. I was as anxious to leave as she was. Yet I am not a superstitious man. As proof of it, after the first effect of these events had left me, I began to question my first impressions and feel tolerably ashamed of my past credulity. Though the phenomenon we had observed could not to all appearance be explained by any natural hypothesis; though I had seen, and my wife had seen, a strange woman suddenly become visible in a room which a moment before had held no one but ourselves, and into which no live woman could have entered without our knowledge, something—was it my natural good sense?—recoiled before a supernatural explanation of this, and I found myself forced to believe that our first visitor had been as real as the last; in other words, the same woman.

But could I prove it? Could the seemingly impossible be made possible and the unexplainable receive a solution satisfying to a rational mind? I determined to make an effort to accomplish this, if only to relieve the mind of my wife, who had not recovered her equanimity as readily as myself.

Starting with the assumption above mentioned—that the woman who had died in our presence was the same who had previously found an unexplainable entrance into these same rooms—I first inquired if the black cloak lined with gray did not offer a solution to some of my previous difficulties. It was a long cloak, enveloping her completely. When worn with the black side out, she would present an inconspicuous appearance, but with the gray side out and the effect of this heightened by a long gray veil flung over her hat, she would look like the gray lady I had first seen. Now, a cloak can be turned in an instant, and if she had chosen to do this in flitting through my door I would naturally find only a sedate, black-clothed woman passing up the street, when, rousing from the apathy into which her appearance had thrown me, I rushed to the front door and looked out. Had I seen such a woman? I seemed to remember that I had. Thus much, then, was satisfactory, but to account for her entrance into our rooms was not so easy. Had she slipped by me in coming in as she had on going out? The parlor door was open, for I had been out to get the paper. Could she have glided in by me unperceived and thus have found her way into the bedroom from which I afterward saw her issue? No, for I had stood facing the front hall door all the time. Through the bedroom door then? But that was, as I have said, locked. Here was a mystery, then; but it was one worth solving.

My first step was to recall all that I had heard of the actual woman who had been buried from our rooms. Her name, as ascertained in the cheap boarding-house to which she was traced, was Helmuth, and she was, so far as any one knew, without friends or relatives in the city. To those who saw her daily she was a harmless, slightly demented woman with money enough to live above want, but not enough to warrant her boasting talk about the rich things she was going to buy some day and the beautiful presents she would soon be in a position to give away. The money found on her person was sufficient to bury her, but no papers were in her possession, nor any letters calculated to throw light upon her past life.

Her lameness had been caused by paralysis, but the date of her attack was not known.

Finding no clue in this to what I wished to learn, I went back to our old rooms, which had not been let since our departure, and sought for one there, and, strangely enough, I found it. I thought I knew everything there was to be known about the apartment we had lived in two months, but one little fact had escaped me which, under the scrutiny that I now gave it, became apparent. This was simply that the key which opened the hall door of the bedroom and which we had seldom if ever used was not as old a key as that of the corresponding door in the parlor, and this fact, small as it was, led me to make inquiries.

The result was that I learned something about the couple who had preceded us in the use of these rooms. They were of middle age and of great personal elegance, but uncertain pay, the husband being nothing more nor less than a professional gambler. Their name was L'Hommedieu.

When I first heard of them, I thought that Mrs. L'Hommedieu might be the Mrs. Helmuth in whose history I was so interested, but from all I could learn she was a very different sort of person. Mrs. L'Hommedieu was gay, dashing and capable of making a show out of a flimsy silk a shop-girl would hesitate to wear. Yet she looked distinguished and wore her cheap jewelry with more grace than many a woman her diamonds. I would, consequently, have dropped this inquiry if some one had not remarked upon her having had a paralytic stroke after leaving the house. This, together with the fact that the key to the rear door, which I had found replaced by a new one, had been taken away by her and never returned, connected her so indubitably with my mysterious visitor that I resolved to pursue my investigations into Mrs. L'Hommedieu's past.

For this purpose I sought out a quaint little maiden-lady living on the top floor, who, I was told, knew more about the L'Hommedieus' than any one in the building. Miss Winterburn, whose acquaintance I had failed to make while residing in the house, was a fluttering, eager, affable person, whose one delight was, as I soon found, to talk about the L'Hommedieus'. Of the story she related I give as much as I can of it in her own words.

"I was never their equal," said she, "but Mrs. L'Hommedieu was lonely, and, having no friends in town, was good enough to admit me to her parlor now and then and even to allow me to accompany her to the theater when her husband was away on one of his mysterious visits. I never liked Mr. L'Hommedieu, but I did like her. She was so different from me, and, when I first knew her, so gay and so full of conversation. But after awhile she changed and was either feverishly cheerful or morbidly sad, so that my visits caused me more pain than pleasure. The reason for these changes in her was patent to everybody. Though her husband was a handsome man, he was as unprincipled as he was unfortunate. He gambled. This she once admitted to me, and while at long intervals he met with some luck he more often returned dispirited and with that hungry, ravening look you expect to see in a wolf cheated of its prey.

"I used to be afraid he would strike her after some one of these disappointments, but I do not think he ever did. She had a determined character of her own, and there have been times when I have thought he was as much afraid of her as she was of him. I became sure of this after one night. Mrs. L'Hommedieu and myself were having a little supper together in the front parlor you have so lately occupied. It was a very ordinary supper, for the L'Hommedieus' purse had run low, and Mrs. L'Hommedieu was not the woman to spend much at any time on her eating. It was palatable, however, and had been cooked by us both together, and I was enjoying it and would have enjoyed it more if Mrs. L'Hommedieu had had more appetite. But she ate scarcely anything and seemed very anxious and unhappy, though she laughed now and then with sudden gusts of mirth too hysterical to be real. It was not late, and yet we were both very much surprised when there came a knock at the door, followed by the entrance of a visitor.

"Mrs. L'Hommedieu, who is always la grande dame, rose without apparent embarrassment to meet the gentleman who entered, though I knew she could not help but feel keenly the niggardly appearance of the board she left with such grace. The stranger—he was certainly a stranger; this I could see by the formality of her manner—was a gentleman of urbane bearing and a general air of prosperity.

"I remember every word that passed.

"'My name is Lafarge,' said he. 'I am, or rather have been, under great obligations to your husband, and I have come to discharge my debt. Is he at home?'

"Mrs. L'Hommedieu's eye, which had sparkled at his name, dropped suddenly as he put the final question.

"'I am sorry,' she returned after a moment of embarrassment, 'but my husband is very seldom home evenings. If you could come about noon some day'—

"'Thank you,' said he, with a bright smile, 'but I will finish my business now and with you, seeing that Mr. L'Hommedieu is not at home. Years ago—I am sure you have heard your husband mention my name—I borrowed quite a sum of money from him, which I have never paid. You recall the amount, no doubt?'

"'I have heard Mr. L'Hommedieu say it was a thousand dollars,' she replied, with a sudden fluttering of her hands indicative of great excitement.

"'That is the sum,' he allowed, either not noticing me or thinking me too insignificant to be considered. 'I regret to have kept him so long out of it, but I have not forgotten to add the interest in making out this statement of my indebtedness, and if you will look over this paper and acknowledge its correctness I will leave the equivalent of my debt here and now, for I sail for Europe to-morrow morning and wish to have all my affairs in order before leaving.'

"Mrs. L'Hommedieu, who looked ready to faint from excess of feeling, summoned up her whole strength, looking so beautiful as she did so, that one forgot the ribbons on her sleeves were no longer fresh and that the silk dress she wore hung in the very limpest of folds.

"'I am obliged to you,' she said in a tone from which she strove in vain to suppress all eagerness. 'And if I may speak for Mr. L'Hommedieu he will be as grateful for your remembrance of us as for the money you so kindly offer to return to him.'

"The stranger bowed low and took out a folded paper, which he handed her. He was not deceived, I am sure, by her grand airs, and knew as well as I did that no woman ever stood in greater need of money. But nothing in his manner betrayed this knowledge.

"'It is a bond I give you,' he now explained. 'As you will see, it has coupons attached to it, which you can cash at any time. It will prove as valuable to you as so much ready money and possibly more convenient.'

"And with just this hint, which I took as significant of his complete understanding of her position, he took her receipt and politely left the house.

"Once alone with me who am nobody, her joy had full vent. I have never seen any one so lost in delight as she was for a few minutes. To have this money thrust upon her just at a moment when actual want seemed staring her in the face was too much of a relief for her to conceal either the misery she had been under or the satisfaction she now enjoyed. Under the gush of her emotions her whole history came out, but as you have often heard the like I will not repeat it, especially as it was all contained in the cry with which a little later she thrust the bond toward me.

"'He must not see it! He must not! It would go like all the rest, and I would again be left without a cent. Take it and keep it, for I have no means of concealing it here. He is too suspicious.'

"But this was asking more than I was willing to grant. Seeing how I felt, she thrust the paper into her bosom with a look before which I secretly recoiled. 'You will not charge yourself with such a responsibility?' said she. 'But I can trust you not to tell him?'

"'Yes,' I nodded, feeling sick of the whole business.

"'Then'—But here the door was violently flung open and without any warning Mr. L'Hommedieu burst into the room in a state of as much excitement as his wife, only his was the excitement of desperation.

"'Gone! Gone!' he cried, ignoring me as completely as had Mr. Lafarge. 'Not a dollar left; not even my studs! See!' And he pointed to his shirt front hanging apart in a way I would never have looked for in this reckless but fastidious gentleman. 'Yet if I had had a dollar more or even a ring worth a dollar or so I might have—Theresa, have you any money at all? A coin now might save us.'

"Mrs. L'Hommedieu, who had turned alarmingly pale, drew up her fine figure and resolutely confronted him. 'No!' said she, and shifting her gaze she turned it meaningly upon me.

"He misunderstood this movement. Thinking it simply a reminder of my presence, he turned and, with his false but impressive show of courtesy, made me a low bow. Then he forgot me utterly again, and facing his wife, growled out:

"'Where are you going to get breakfast then? You don't look like a woman who expects to starve!'

"It was a fatal remark, for, do what she would, she could not prevent a slight smile of disdain, and, seeing it, he kept his eyes riveted on her face till her uneasiness became manifest. Instantly his suspicion took form, and, surveying her still more fixedly, he espied a corner of the precious paper protruding slightly above her corsage. To snatch it out, open it and realize its value was the work of a moment. Her cry of dismay and his shout of mad triumph rang out simultaneously, and never have I seen such an ebullition of opposing passions as I was made witness to as his hand closed over this small fortune and their staring eyes met in the mortal struggle they had now entered upon for its ultimate possession.

"She was the first to speak. 'It was given to me; it was meant for me. If I keep it, both of us will profit by it, but if you—'

"He did not wait for her to finish. 'Where did you get it?' he cried. 'I can break the bank with what I can raise on this bond at the club. Darraugh's in town. You know what that means. Luck's in the air, and with an hundred dollars—But I've no time to talk. I came for a dollar, a fifty-cent piece, a dime even, and I go back with a bond worth—'

"But she was already between him and the door. 'You will never carry that bond out of this house,' she whispered in the tone which goes further than any cry. 'I have not held it in my hand to see it follow every other good thing I have had in life. I will not, Henry. Take that bond and sink it as you have all the rest and I fall at your feet a dead woman. I will never survive the destruction of my last hope.'

"He was cowed—for a moment, that is; she looked so superb and so determined. Then all that was mean and despicable in his thinly veneered nature came to the surface, and, springing forward with an oath, he was about to push her aside, when, without the moving of a finger on her part, he reeled back, recovered himself, caught at a chair, missed it and fell heavily to the floor.

"'My God, I thank thee!' was the exclamation with which she broke from the trance of terror into which she had been thrown by his sudden attempt to pass her; and without a glance at his face, which to me looked like the face of a dead man, she tore the paper from his hand and stood looking about her with a wild and searching gaze, in the desperate hope that somehow the walls would open and offer her a safe place of concealment for the precious sheet of paper. Meanwhile I had crept near the prostrate man. He was breathing, but was perfectly unconscious.

"'Don't you mean to do something for him?' I asked. 'He may die.'

"She met my question with the dazed air of one suddenly awakened. 'No, he'll not die, but he'll not come to for some minutes, and this must be hidden first. But where? where? I cannot trust it on my person or in any place a man like him would search. I must devise some means—ah!'

"With this final exclamation she had dashed into the other room. I did not see where she went—I did not want to—but I soon realized she was working somewhere in a desperate hurry. I could hear her breath coming in quick, short pants as I bent over her husband, waiting for him to rouse and hating my inaction even while I succumbed to it.

"Suddenly she was back in the parlor again, and to my surprise passed immediately to the little table in the corner where we had sat at supper. We had had for our simple refreshment that homeliest of all dishes, boiled milk thickened with flour. There was still some left in a bowl, and taking this away with her, she called back hoarsely:

"'Pray that he does not come to till I have finished. It will be the best prayer you ever made.'

"She told me afterward that he was subject to these attacks and that she had long ceased to be alarmed by them. But to me the sight of this man lying there so helpless, was horrible and, though I hated him and pitied her, I scarcely knew what to wish. While battling with my desire to run and the feeling of loyalty which held me kneeling at that man's side, I heard her speak again, this time in an even and slightly hard tone: 'Now you may dash a glass of cold water in his face. I am prepared to meet him. Happily his memory fails him after these attacks. I may succeed in making him believe that the bond he saw was one of his fancies.'

"'Had you not better throw the water yourself?' I suggested, getting up and meeting her eye very quietly.

"She looked at me in wonder, then moved calmly to the table, took the glass and dashed a few drops of water into her husband's face. Instantly he began to stir, seeing which I arose without haste, but without any unnecessary delay, and quietly took my leave. I could bear no more that night.

"Next morning I awoke in a fright. I had dreamed that he had come to my room in search of the bond. But it was only her knock at the door and her voice, asking if she might enter at this early hour. It was such a relief I gladly let her in, and she entered with her best air and flung herself on my little lounge with the hysterical cry:

"'He has sent me up. I told him I ought not to intrude at such an inconvenient hour: that you would not have had your breakfast.' (How carelessly she spoke! How hard she tried to keep the hungry note out of her voice!) 'But he insisted upon my coming up. I know why. He searched me before I left the room, and now he wants to search the room itself.'

"'Then he did remember?' I began.

"'Yes, he remembers now. I saw it in his eyes as soon as he awoke. But he will not find the bond. That is safe, and some day when I shall have escaped his vigilance long enough to get it back again I will use it so as to make him as well as myself comfortable. I am not a selfish woman.'

"I did not think she was, and I felt pity for her, and so after dressing and making her a cup of tea—I can myself do very well without one on a pinch—I sat down with her, and we chatted for an hour or so quite comfortably. Then she grew so restless and consulted the clock so often that I tried to soothe her by remarking that it was not an easy task he had set himself, at which she laughed in a mysterious way, but failed to grow less anxious till our suspense was cut short by the appearance of the janitor with a message from Mr. L'Hommedieu.

"'Mr. L'Hommedieu's compliments,' said he, 'and he hopes Mrs. L'Hommedieu will make herself comfortable and not think of coming down. He is doing everything that is necessary and will soon be through. You can rest quite easy, ma'am.'

"'What does he mean?' marveled the poor woman as the janitor disappeared. 'Is he spending all this time ransacking the rooms? I wish I dared disobey him. I wish I dared go down.'

"But her courage was not equal to an open disregard of his wishes, and she had to subdue her impatience and wait for a summons that did not come till near two o'clock. Then Mr. L'Hommedieu himself appeared with her hat and mantle on his arm.

"'My dear,' said he as she rose, haggard with excitement, to meet him, 'I have brought your wraps with me that you may go directly from here to our new home. Shall I assist you to put them on? You do not look as well as usual, and that is why I have undertaken this thing all myself—to save you, my dear; to save you each and every exertion.'

"I had flung out my arms to catch her, for I thought she was going to faint, but she did not, though I think it would have been better for her if she had.

"'We are going to leave this house?' she asked, speaking very slowly and with a studied lack of emotion that imposed upon nobody.

"'I have said so,' he smiled. 'The dray has already taken away the half of our effects, and the rest will follow at Mrs. Latimer's convenience.'

"'Ah, I understand!' she replied, with a gasp of relief significant of her fear that by some superhuman cunning he had found the bond she thought so safely concealed. 'I was wondering how Mrs. Latimer came to allow us to leave.' (I tell you they always talked as if I were not present.) 'Our goods are left as a surety, it seems.'

"'Half of our goods,' he blandly corrected. 'Would it interest you to know which half?'

"'The cunning of this insinuation was matched by the imperturbable shrug with which she replied. 'So a bed has been allowed us and some clothes I am satisfied,' at which he bit his lips, vexed at her self-control and his own failure to break it.

"'You have not asked where we are going,' he observed as with apparent solicitude he threw her mantle over her shoulders.

"The air of lassitude with which she replied bespoke her feeling on that point. 'I have little curiosity,' she said. 'You know I can be happy anywhere. And, turning toward me, she moved her lips in a way I interpreted to mean: 'Go below with me. See me out.'

"'Say what you have to say to Miss Winter-burn aloud,' he dryly suggested.

"'I have nothing to say to Miss Winterburn but thanks,' was her cold reply, belied, however, by the trembling of her fingers as she essayed to fit on her gloves.

"'And those I will receive below!' I cried, with affected gaiety. 'I am going down with you to the door.' And resolutely ignoring his frown I tripped down before them. On the last stair I felt her steps lagging. Instantly I seemed to comprehend what was required of me, and, rushing forward, I entered the front parlor. He followed close behind me, for how could he know I was not in collusion with her to regain the bond? This gave her one minute by herself in the rear, and in that minute she secured the key which would give her future access to the spot where her treasure lay hidden.

"The rest of the story I must give you mainly from hearsay. You must understand by this time what Mr. L'Hommedieu's scheme was in moving thus suddenly. He knew that it would be impossible for him, by the most minute and continuous watchfulness, to prevent his wife from recovering the bond while they continued to inhabit the rooms in which, notwithstanding his failure to find it, he had reason to believe it still lay concealed. But once in other quarters it would be comparatively easy for him to subject her to a surveillance which not only would prevent her from returning to this house without his knowledge, but would lead her to give away her secret by the very natural necessity she would be under of going to the exact spot where her treasure lay hid.

"It was a cunning plot and showed him to be as able as he was unscrupulous. How it worked I will now proceed to tell you. It must have been the next afternoon that the janitor came running up to me—I suppose he had learned by this time that I had more than ordinary interest in these people—to say that Mrs. L'Hommedieu had been in the house and had been so frightened by a man who had followed her that she had fainted dead away on the floor. Would I go down to her?

"I had rather have gone anywhere else, unless it was to prison, but duty cannot be shirked, and I followed the man down. But we were too late. Mrs. L'Hommedieu had recovered and gone away, and the person who had frightened her was also gone, and only the hall-boy remained to give any explanations.

"This was what he had to say:

"'The man it was who went first. As soon as the lady fell he skipped out. I don't think he meant no good here—'

"'Did she drop here in the hall?' I asked, unable to restrain my intense anxiety.

"'Oh, no, ma'am! They was in the back room yonder, which she got in somehow. The man followed her in, sneaking and sneaking like an eel or a cop, and she fell right against—'

"'Don't tell me where!' I cried. 'I don't want to know where!' And I was about to return up-stairs when I heard a quick, sharp voice behind me and realized that Mr. L'Hommedieu had come in and was having some dispute with the janitor.

"Common prudence led me to listen. He wanted, as was very natural, to enter the room where his wife had just been surprised, but the janitor, alarmed by the foregoing very irregular proceedings, was disposed to deny his right to do so.

"'The furniture is held as a surety,' said he, 'and I have orders—'

"But Mr. L'Hommedieu had a spare dollar, and before many minutes had elapsed I heard him go into that room and close the door. Of the next ten minutes and the suspense I felt I need not speak. When he came out again, he looked as if the ground would not hold him.

"'I have done some mischief, I fear,' he airily said as he passed by the janitor. 'But I'll pay for it. Don't worry. I'll pay for it and the rent, too, to-morrow. You may tell Mrs. Latimer so.' And he was gone, leaving us all agape in the hallway.

"A minute later we all crept to that room and looked in. Now that he had got the money I for one was determined to know where she had hid it. There was no mistaking the spot. A single glance was enough to show us the paper ripped off from a portion of the wall, revealing a narrow gap behind the baseboard large enough to hold the bond. It was near—"

"Wait!" I put in as I remembered where the so called Mrs. Helmuth had pointed just before she died. "Wasn't it at the left of the large folding doors and midway to the wall?"

"How came you to know?" she asked. "Did Mrs. Latimer tell you?" But as I did not answer she soon took up the thread of her narrative again, and, sighing softly, said:

"The next day came and went, but no Mr. L'Hommedieu appeared; another, and I began to grow seriously uneasy; a third, and a dreadful thing happened. Late in the afternoon Mrs. L'Hommedieu, dressed very oddly for her, came sliding in at the front door, and with an appealing smile at the hall-boy, who wished but dared not ask her for the key which made these visits possible, glided by to her old rooms, and, finding the door unlocked, went softly in. Her appearance is worth description, for it shows the pitiful efforts she made at disguise, in the hope, I suppose, of escaping the surveillance she was evidently conscious of being under. She was in the habit of wearing on cool days a black circular with a gray lining. This she had turned inside out so that the gray was uppermost, while over her neat black bonnet she had flung a long veil, also gray, which not only hid her face, but gave to her appearance an eccentric look as different as possible from her usual aspect. The hall-boy, who had never seen her save in showy black or bright colors, said she looked like a ghost in the daytime, but it was all done for a purpose, I am sure, and to escape the attention of the man who had before followed her. Alas, he might have followed her this time without addition to her suffering! Scarcely had she entered the room where her treasure had been left than she saw the torn paper and gaping baseboard, and, uttering a cry so piercing it found its way even to the stolid heart of the hall-boy, she tottered back into the hall, where she fell into the arms of her husband, who had followed her in from the street in a state of frenzy almost equal to her own.

"The janitor, who that minute appeared on the stairway, says that he never saw two such faces. They looked at each other and were speechless. He was the first to hang his head.

"'It is gone, Henry,' she whispered. 'It is gone. You have taken it.'

"He did not answer.

"'And it is lost! You have risked it, and it is lost!'

"He uttered a groan. 'You should have given it to me that night. There was luck in the air then. Now the devil is in the cards and—'

"Her arms went up with a shriek. 'My curse be upon you, Henry L'Hommedieu!' And whether it was the look with which she said this that moved him, or whether there was some latent love in his heart for this once beautiful and long-suffering woman, he shrank at her words, and, stumbling like a man in the darkness, uttered a heart-rending groan and rushed from the house. We never saw him again.

"As for her, she fell this time under a paralytic attack which robbed her of her faculties. She was taken to a hospital, where I frequently visited her, but either from grief or the effect of her attack she did not know me, nor did she ever recognize any of us again. Mrs. Latimer, who is a just woman, sold her furniture and after paying herself out of the proceeds, gave the remainder to the hospital nurses in charge for Mrs. L'Hommedieu, so that when she left there she had something with which to start life anew. But where she went or how she managed to get along in her enfeebled condition I do not know. I never heard of her again."

"Then you did not see the woman who died in those rooms?" I asked.

The effect of these words was magical and led to mutual explanations. She had not seen that woman, having encountered all the sorrow she wished to in that room. Nor was there any one else in the house who would be likely to recognize Mrs. L'Hommedieu; both the janitor and hall-boy being new and Mrs. Latimer one of those proprietors who are only seen on rent day. For the rest, Mrs. L'Hommedieu's defective memory, which had led her to haunt the house and room where her money had once been hidden, accounted not only for her first visit, but the last, which had ended so fatally. The cunning she showed in turning her cloak and flinging a veil over her hat was the cunning of a partially clouded mind. It was a reminiscence of the morning when her terrible misfortune occurred. My habit of taking the key out of the lock of that unused door made the use of her own key possible, and her fear of being followed, caused her to lock the door behind her. My wife, who must have fallen into a doze on my leaving her, did not see her enter, but detected her just as she was trying to escape through the folding doors. My presence in the parlor probably added to her embarrassment, and she fled, turning her cloak as she did so.

How simple it seemed now that we knew the facts; but how obscure, and to all appearance, unexplainable, before the clew was given to the mystery!

MIDNIGHT IN BEAUCHAMP ROW

It was the last house in Beauchamp Row, and it stood several rods away from its nearest neighbor. It was a pretty house in the daytime, but owing to its deep, sloping roof and small bediamonded windows it had a lonesome look at night, notwithstanding the crimson hall-light which shone through the leaves of its vine-covered doorway.

Ned Chivers lived in it with his six months' married bride, and as he was both a busy fellow and a gay one there were many evenings when pretty Letty Chivers sat alone until near midnight.

She was of an uncomplaining spirit, however, and said little, though there were times when both the day and evening seemed very long and married life not altogether the paradise she had expected.

On this evening—a memorable evening for her, the twenty-fourth of December, 1894—she had expected her husband to remain with her, for it was not only Christmas eve, but the night when, as manager of a large manufacturing concern, he brought up from New York the money with which to pay off the men on the next working day, and he never left her when there was any unusual amount of money in the house. But from the first glimpse she had of him coming up the road she knew she was to be disappointed in this hope, and, indignant, alarmed almost, at the prospect of a lonesome evening under these circumstances, she ran hastily down to the gate to meet him, crying:

"Oh, Ned, you look so troubled I know you have only come home for a hurried supper. But you cannot leave me to-night. Tennie" (their only maid) "has gone for a holiday, and I never can stay in this house alone with all that." She pointed to the small bag he carried, which, as she knew, was filled to bursting with bank notes.

He certainly looked troubled. It is hard to resist the entreaty in a young bride's uplifted face. But this time he could not help himself, and he said:

"I am dreadful sorry, but I must ride over to Fairbanks to-night. Mr. Pierson has given me an imperative order to conclude a matter of business there, and it is very important that it should be done. I should lose my position if I neglected the matter, and no one but Hasbrouck and Suffern knows that we keep the money in the house. I have always given out that I intrusted it to Hale's safe overnight."

"But I cannot stand it," she persisted. "You have never left me on these nights. That is why I let Tennie go. I will spend the evening at The Larches, or, better still, call in Mr. and Mrs. Talcott to keep me company."

But her husband did not approve of her going out or of her having company. The Larches was too far away, and as for Mr. and Mrs. Talcott, they were meddlesome people, whom he had never liked; besides, Mrs. Talcott was delicate, and the night threatened storm. It seemed hard to subject her to this ordeal, and he showed that he thought so by his manner, but, as circumstances were, she would have to stay alone, and he only hoped she would be brave and go to bed like a good girl, and think nothing about the money, which he would take care to put away in a very safe place.

"Or," said he, kissing her downcast face, "perhaps you would rather hide it yourself; women always have curious ideas about such things."

"Yes, let me hide it," she murmured. "The money, I mean, not the bag. Every one knows the bag. I should never dare to leave it in that." And begging him to unlock it, she began to empty it with a feverish haste that rather alarmed him, for he surveyed her anxiously and shook his head as if he dreaded the effects of this excitement upon her.

But as he saw no way of averting it he confined himself to using such soothing words as were at his command, and then, humoring her weakness, helped her to arrange the bills in the place she had chosen, and restuffing the bag with old receipts till it acquired its former dimensions, he put a few bills on top to make the whole look natural, and, laughing at her white face, relocked the bag and put the key back in his pocket.

"There, dear; a notable scheme and one that should relieve your mind entirely!" he cried. "If any one should attempt burglary in my absence and should succeed in getting into a house as safely locked as this will be when I leave it, then trust to their being satisfied when they see this booty, which I shall hide where I always hide it—in the cupboard over my desk."

"And when will you be back?" she murmured, trembling in spite of herself at these preparations.

"By one o'clock if possible. Certainly by two."

"And our neighbors go to bed at ten," she murmured. But the words were low, and she was glad he did not hear them, for if it was his duty to obey the orders he had received, then it was her duty to meet the position in which it left her as bravely as she could.

At supper she was so natural that his face rapidly brightened, and it was with quite an air of cheerfulness that he rose at last to lock up the house and make such preparations as were necessary for his dismal ride over the mountains to Fairbanks. She had the supper dishes to wash up in Tennie's absence, and as she was a busy little housewife she found herself singing a snatch of song as she passed back and forth from dining-room to kitchen. He heard it, too, and smiled to himself as he bolted the windows on the ground floor and examined the locks of the three lower doors, and when he finally came into the kitchen with his greatcoat on to give her his final kiss, he had but one parting injunction to urge, and that was that she should lock the front door after him and then forget the whole matter till she heard his double knock at midnight.

She smiled and held up her ingenuous face.

"Be careful of yourself," she murmured. "I hate this dark ride for you, and on such a night too." And she ran with him to the door to look out.

"It is certainly very dark," he responded, "but I'm to have one of Brown's safest horses. Do not worry about me. I shall do well enough, and so will you, too, or you are not the plucky little woman I have always thought you."

She laughed, but there was a choking sound in her voice that made him look at her again. But at sight of his anxiety she recovered herself, and pointing to the clouds said earnestly:

"It is going to snow. Be careful as you ride by the gorge, Ned; it is very deceptive there in a snowstorm."

But he vowed that it would not snow before morning, and giving her one final embrace he dashed down the path toward Brown's livery stable. "Oh, what is the matter with me?" she murmured to herself as his steps died out in the distance. "I never knew I was such a coward." And she paused for a moment, looking up and down the road, as if in despite of her husband's command she had the desperate idea of running away to some neighbor.

But she was too loyal for that, and smothering a sigh she retreated into the house. As she did so the first flakes fell of the storm that was not to have come till morning.

It took her an hour to get her kitchen in order, and nine o'clock struck before she was ready to sit down. She had been so busy she had not noticed how the wind had increased or how rapidly the snow was falling. But when she went to the front door for another glance up and down the road she started back, appalled at the fierceness of the gale and at the great pile of snow that had already accumulated on the doorstep.

Too delicate to breast such a wind, she saw herself robbed of her last hope of any companionship, and sighing heavily she locked and bolted the door for the night and went back into her little sitting-room, where a great fire was burning. Here she sat down, and determined, now that she must pass the evening alone, to do it as cheerfully as possible, and so began to sew. "Oh, what a Christmas eve!" she thought, and a picture of other homes rose before her eyes, homes in which husbands sat by wives and brothers by sisters, and a great wave of regret poured over her and a longing for something, she hardly dared say what, lest her unhappiness should acquire a sting that would leave traces beyond the passing moment. The room in which she sat was the only one on the ground floor except the dining-room and kitchen. It therefore was used both as parlor and sitting-room, and held not only her piano, but her husband's desk.

Communicating with it was the tiny dining-room. Between the two, however, was an entry leading to a side entrance. A lamp was in this entry, and she had left it burning, as well as the one in the kitchen, that the house might look cheerful and as if all the family were at home.

She was looking toward this entry and wondering whether it was the mist made by her tears that made it look so dismally dark to her when there came a faint sound from the door at its further end.

Knowing that her husband must have taken peculiar pains with the fastenings of this door, as it was the one toward the woods and therefore most accessible to wayfarers, she sat where she was, with all her faculties strained to listen. But no further sound came from that direction, and after a few minutes of silent terror she was allowing herself to believe that she had been deceived by her fears when she suddenly heard the same sound at the kitchen door, followed by a muffled knock.

Frightened now in good earnest, but still alive to the fact that the intruder was as likely to be a friend as a foe, she stepped to the door, and with her hand on the lock stooped and asked boldly enough who was there. But she received no answer, and more affected by this unexpected silence than by the knock she had heard she recoiled farther and farther till not only the width of the kitchen, but the dining-room also, lay between her and the scene of her alarm, when to her utter confusion the noise shifted again to the side of the house, and the door she thought so securely fastened, swung violently open as if blown in by a fierce gust, and she saw precipitated into the entry the burly figure of a man covered with snow and shaking with the violence of the storm that seemed at once to fill the house.

Her first thought was that it was her husband come back, but before she could clear her eyes from the cloud of snow which had entered with him he had thrown off his outer covering and she found herself face to face with a man in whose powerful frame and cynical visage she saw little to comfort her and much to surprise and alarm.

"Ugh!" was his coarse and rather familiar greeting. "A hard night, missus! Enough to drive any man indoors. Pardon the liberty, but I couldn't wait for you to lift the latch; the wind drove me right in."

"Was—was not the door locked?" she feebly asked, thinking he must have staved it in with his foot, that looked only too well fitted for such a task.

"Not much," he chuckled. "I s'pose you're too hospitable for that." And his eyes passed from her face to the comfortable firelight shining through the sitting-room.

"Is it refuge you want?" she demanded, suppressing as much as possible all signs of fear.

"Sure, missus—what else! A man can't live in a gale like that, specially after a tramp of twenty miles or more. Shall I shut the door for you?" he asked, with a mixture of bravado and good nature that frightened her more and more.

"I will shut it," she replied, with a half notion of escaping this sinister stranger by a flight through the night.

But one glance into the swirling snow-storm deterred her, and making the best of the alarming situation, she closed the door, but did not lock it, being more afraid now of what was inside the house than of anything left to threaten her from without.

The man, whose clothes were dripping with water, watched her with a cynical smile, and then, without any invitation, entered the dining-room, crossed it and moved toward the kitchen fire.

"Ugh! ugh! But it is warm here!" he cried, his nostrils dilating with an animal-like enjoyment that in itself was repugnant to her womanly delicacy. "Do you know, missus, I shall have to stay here all night? Can't go out in that gale again; not such a fool." Then with a sly look at her trembling form and white face he insinuatingly added, "All alone, missus?"

The suddenness with which this was put, together with the leer that accompanied it, made her start. Alone? Yes, but should she acknowledge it? Would it not be better to say that her husband was upstairs. The man evidently saw the struggle going on in her mind, for he chuckled to himself and called out quite boldly:

"Never mind, missus; it's all right. Just give me a bit of cold meat and a cup of tea or something, and we'll be very comfortable together. You're a slender slip of a woman to be minding a house like this. I'll keep you company if you don't mind, leastwise until the storm lets up a bit, which ain't likely for some hours to come. Rough night, missus, rough night."

"I expect my husband home at any time," she hastened to say. And thinking she saw a change in the man's countenance at this she put on quite an air of sudden satisfaction and bounded toward the front of the house. "There! I think I hear him now," she cried.

Her motive was to gain time, and if possible to obtain the opportunity of shifting the money from the place where she had first put it into another and safer one. "I want to be able," she thought, "of swearing that I have no money with me in this house. If I can only get it into my apron I will drop it outside the door into the snowbank. It will be as safe there as in the bank it came from." And dashing into the sitting-room she made a feint of dragging down a shawl from a screen, while she secretly filled her skirt with the bills which had been put between some old pamphlets on the bookshelves.

She could hear the man grumbling in the kitchen, but he did not follow her front, and taking advantage of the moment's respite from his none too encouraging presence she unbarred the door and cheerfully called out her husband's name.

The ruse was successful. She was enabled to fling the notes where the falling flakes would soon cover them from sight, and feeling more courageous, now that the money was out of the house, she went slowly back, saying she had made a mistake, and that it was the wind she had heard.

The man gave a gruff but knowing guffaw and then resumed his watch over her, following her steps as she proceeded to set him out a meal, with a persistency that reminded her of a tiger just on the point of springing. But the inviting look of the viands with which she was rapidly setting the table soon distracted his attention, and allowing himself one grunt of satisfaction, he drew up a chair and set himself down to what to him was evidently a most savory repast.

"No beer? No ale? Nothing o' that sort, eh? Don't keep a bar?" he growled, as his teeth closed on a huge hunk of bread.

She shook her head, wishing she had a little cold poison bottled up in a tight-looking jug.

"Nothing but tea," she smiled, astonished at her own ease of manner in the presence of this alarming guest.

"Then let's have that," he grumbled, taking the bowl she handed him, with an odd look that made her glad to retreat to the other side of the room.

"Jest listen to the howling wind," he went on between the huge mouthfuls of bread and cheese with which he was gorging himself. "But we're very comfortable, we two! We don't mind the storm, do we?"

Shocked by his familiarity and still more moved by the look of mingled inquiry and curiosity with which his eyes now began to wander over the walls and cupboards, she took an anxious step toward the side of the house looking toward her neighbors, and lifting one of the shades, which had all been religiously pulled down, she looked out. A swirl of snow-flakes alone confronted her. She could neither see her neighbors, nor could she be seen by them. A shout from her to them would not be heard. She was as completely isolated as if the house stood in the center of a desolate western plain.

"I have no trust but in God," she murmured as she came from the window. And, nerved to meet her fate, she crossed to the kitchen.

It was now half-past ten. Two hours and a half must elapse before her husband could possibly arrive.

She set her teeth at the thought and walked resolutely into the room.

"Are you done?" she asked.

"I am, ma'am," he leered. "Do you want me to wash the dishes? I kin, and I will." And he actually carried his plate and cup to the sink, where he turned the water upon them with another loud guffaw.

"If only his fancy would take him into the pantry," she thought, "I could shut and lock the door upon him and hold him prisoner till Ned gets back."

But his fancy ended its flight at the sink, and before her hopes had fully subsided he was standing on the threshold of the sitting-room door.

"It's pretty here," he exclaimed, allowing his eye to rove again over every hiding-place within sight. "I wonder now"—He stopped. His glance had fallen on the cupboard over her husband's desk.

"Well?" she asked, anxious to break the thread of his thought, which was only too plainly mirrored in his eager countenance.

He started, dropped his eyes, and turning looked at her with a momentary fierceness. But, as she did not let her own glance quail, but continued to look at him with what she meant for a smile on her pale lips, he subdued this outward manifestation of passion, and, chuckling to hide his embarrassment, began backing into the entry, leering in evident enjoyment of the fears he caused, with what she felt was a most horrible smile. Once in the hall, he hesitated, however, for a long time; then he slowly went toward the garment he had dropped on entering and stooping, drew from underneath its folds a wicked-looking stick. Giving a kick to the coat, which sent it into a remote corner, he bestowed upon her another smile, and still carrying the stick went slowly and reluctantly away into the kitchen.

"Oh, God Almighty, help me!" was her prayer.

There was nothing for her to do now but endure, so throwing herself into a chair, she tried to calm the beating of her heart and summon up courage for the struggle which she felt was before her. That he had come to rob and only waited to take her off her guard she now felt certain, and rapidly running over in her mind all the expedients of self-defense possible to one in her situation, she suddenly remembered the pistol which Ned kept in his desk. Oh, why had she not thought of it before! Why had she let herself grow mad with terror when here, within reach of her hand, lay such a means of self-defense? With a feeling of joy (she had always hated pistols before and scolded Ned when he bought this one) she started to her feet and slid her hand into the drawer. But it came back empty. Ned had taken the weapon away with him.

For a moment, a surge of the bitterest feeling she had ever experienced passed over her; then she called reason to her aid and was obliged to acknowledge that the act was but natural, and that from his standpoint he was much more likely to need it than herself. But the disappointment, coming so soon after hope, unnerved her, and she sank back in her chair, giving herself up for lost.

How long she sat there with her eyes on the door, through which she momentarily expected her assailant to reappear, she never knew. She was conscious only of a sort of apathy that made movement difficult and even breathing a task. In vain she tried to change her thoughts. In vain she tried to follow her husband in fancy over the snow-covered roads and into the gorge of the mountains. Imagination failed her at this point. Do what she would, all was misty in her mind's eye, and she could not see that wandering image. There was blankness between his form and her, and no life or movement anywhere but here in the scene of her terror.

Her eyes were on a strip of rug that covered the entry floor, and so strange was the condition of her mind that she found herself mechanically counting the tassels that finished its edge, growing wroth over one that was worn, till she hated that sixth tassel and mentally determined that if she ever outlived this night she would strip them all off and be done with them.

The wind had lessened, but the air had grown cooler and the snow made a sharp sound where it struck the panes. She felt it falling, though she had cut off all view of it. It seemed to her that a pall was settling over the world and that she would soon be smothered under its folds. Meanwhile no sound came from the kitchen, only that dreadful sense of a doom creeping upon her—a sense that grew in intensity till she found herself watching for the shadow of that lifted stick on the wall of the entry, and almost imagined she saw the tip of it appearing, when without any premonition, that fatal side door again blew in and admitted another man of so threatening an aspect that she succumbed instantly before him and forgot all her former fears in this new terror.

The second intruder was a negro of powerful frame and lowering aspect, and as he came for-ward and stood in the doorway there was observable in his fierce and desperate countenance no attempt at the insinuation of the other, only a fearful resolution that made her feel like a puppet before him, and drove her, almost without her volition, to her knees.

"Money? Is it money you want?" was her desperate greeting. "If so, here's my purse and here are my rings and watch. Take them and go."

But the stolid wretch did not even stretch out his hands. His eyes went beyond her, and the mingled anxiety and resolve which he displayed would have cowed a stouter heart than that of this poor woman.

"Keep de trash," he growled. "I want de company's money. You 've got it—two thousand dollars. Show me where it is, that's all, and I won't trouble you long after I close on it."

"But it's not in the house," she cried. "I swear it is not in the house. Do you think Mr. Chivers would leave me here alone with two thousand dollars to guard?"

But the negro, swearing that she lied, leaped into the room, and tearing open the cupboard above her husband's desk, seized the bag from the corner where they had put it.

"He brought it in this," he muttered, and tried to force the bag open, but finding this impossible he took out a heavy knife and cut a big hole in its side. Instantly there fell out the pile of old receipts with which they had stuffed it, and seeing these he stamped with rage, and flinging them in one great handful at her rushed to the drawers below, emptied them, and, finding nothing, attacked the bookcase.

"The money is somewhere here. You can't fool me," he yelled. "I saw the spot your eyes lit on when I first came into the room. Is it behind these books?" he growled, pulling them out and throwing them helter-skelter over the floor. "Women is smart in the hiding business. Is it behind these books, I say?"

They had been, or rather had been placed between the books, but she had taken them away, as we know, and he soon began to realise that his search was bringing him nothing, for leaving the bookcase he gave the books one kick, and seizing her by the arm, shook her with a murderous glare on his strange and distorted features.

"Where's the money?" he hissed. "Tell me, or you are a goner."

He raised his heavy fist. She crouched and all seemed over, when, with a rush and cry, a figure dashed between them and he fell, struck down by the very stick she had so long been expecting to see fall upon her own head. The man who had been her terror for hours had at the moment of need acted as her protector.

She must have fainted, but if so, her unconsciousness was but momentary, for when she again recognized her surroundings she found the tramp still standing over her adversary.

"I hope you don't mind, ma'am," he said, with an air of humbleness she certainly had not seen in him before, "but I think the man's dead." And he stirred with his foot the heavy figure before him.

"Oh, no, no, no!" she cried. "That would be too fearful. He's shocked, stunned; you cannot have killed him."

But the tramp was persistent. "I'm 'fraid I have," he said. "I done it before, and it's been the same every time. But I couldn't see a man of that color frighten a lady like you. My supper was too warm in me, ma'am. Shall I throw him outside the house?"

"Yes," she said, and then, "No; let us first be sure there is no life in him." And, hardly knowing what she did, she stooped down and peered into the glassy eyes of the prostrate man.

Suddenly she turned pale—no, not pale, but ghastly, and cowering back, shook so that the tramp, into whose features a certain refinement had passed since he had acted as her protector, thought she had discovered life in those set orbs, and was stooping down to make sure that this was so, when he saw her suddenly lean forward and, impetuously plunging her hand into the negro's throat, tear open the shirt and give one look at his bared breast.

It was white.

"O God! O God!" she moaned, and lifting the head in her two hands she gave the motionless features a long and searching look. "Water!" she cried. "Bring water." But before the now obedient tramp could respond, she had torn off the woolly wig disfiguring the dead man's head, and seeing the blond curls beneath had uttered such a shriek that it rose above the gale and was heard by her distant neighbors.

It was the head and hair of her husband.

They found out afterwards that he had contemplated this theft for months, that each and every precaution possible to a successful issue to this most daring undertaking had been made use of and that but for the unexpected presence in the house of the tramp, he would doubtless have not only extorted the money from his wife, but have so covered up the deed by a plausible alibi as to have retained her confidence and that of his employers.

Whether the tramp killed him out of sympathy for the defenseless woman or in rage at being disappointed in his own plans has never been determined. Mrs. Chivers herself thinks he was actuated by a rude sort of gratitude.

"In the spring of 1840, the attention of the New York police was attracted by the many cases of well-known men found drowned in the various waters surrounding the lower portion of our great city. Among these may be mentioned the name of Elwood Henderson, the noted tea merchant, whose remains were washed ashore at Redhook Point; and of Christopher Bigelow, who was picked up off Governor's Island after having been in the water for five days, and of another well-known millionaire whose name I cannot now recall, but who, I remember, was seen to walk towards the East River one March evening, and was not met with again till the 5th of April, when his body floated into one of the docks near Peck Slip.

"As it seemed highly improbable that there should have been a concerted action among so many wealthy and distinguished men to end their lives within a few weeks of each other, and all by the same method of drowning, we soon became suspicious that a more serious verdict than that of suicide should have been rendered in the case of Henderson, Bigelow and the other gentleman I have mentioned. Yet one fact, common to all these cases, pointed so conclusively to deliberate intention on the part of the sufferers that we hesitated to take action.

"This was, that upon the body of each of the above-mentioned persons there were found, not only valuables in the shape of money and jewelry, but papers and memoranda of a nature calculated to fix the identity of the drowned man, in case the water should rob him of his personal characteristics. Consequently, we could not ascribe these deaths to a desire for plunder on the part of some unknown person.

"I was a young man in those days, and full of ambition. So, though I said nothing, I did not let this matter drop when the others did, but kept my mind persistently upon it and waited, with odd results as you will hear, for another victim to be reported at police headquarters.

"Meantime I sought to discover some bond or connection between the several men who had been found drowned, which would serve to explain their similar fate. But all my efforts in this direction were fruitless. There was no bond between them, and the matter remained for a while an unsolved mystery.

"Suddenly one morning a clew was placed, not in my hands, but in those of a superior official who at that time exerted a great influence over the whole force. He was sitting in his private room, when there was ushered into his presence a young man of a dissipated but not unprepossessing appearance, who, after a pause of marked embarrassment, entered upon the following story:

"I don't know whether or no, I should offer an excuse for the communication I am about to make; but the matter I have to relate is simply this: Being hard up last night (for though a rich man's son I often lack money), I went to a certain pawn-shop in the Bowery where I had been told I could raise money on my prospects. This place—you may see it sometime, so I will not enlarge upon it—did not strike me favorably; but, being very anxious for a certain definite sum of money, I wrote my name in a book which was brought to me from some unknown quarter, and proceeded to follow the young woman who attended me into what she was pleased to call her good master's private office. He may have been a good master, but he was anything but a good man, In short, sir, when he found out who I was, and how much I needed money, he suggested that I should make an appointment with my father at a place he called Judah's in Grand Street, where, said he, 'your little affair will be arranged, and you made a rich man within thirty days. That is,' he slyly added, 'unless your father has already made a will, disinheriting you.'

"I was shocked, sir, shocked beyond all my powers of concealment, not so much at his words, which I hardly understood, as at his looks, which had a world of evil suggestion in them; so I raised my fist and would have knocked him down, only that I found two young fellows at my elbows, who held me quiet for five minutes, while the old fellow talked to me. He asked me if I came to him on a fool's errand or really to get money; and when I admitted that I had cherished hopes of obtaining a clear two thousand dollars from him, he coolly replied that he knew of but one way in which I could hope to get such an amount, and that if I was too squeamish to adopt it, I had made a mistake in coming to his shop, which was no missionary institution, etc., etc. Not wishing to irritate him, for there was menace in his eye, I asked, with a certain weak show of being sorry for my former heat, whereabouts in Grand Street I should find this Judah. The retort was quick, 'Judah is not his name,' said he, 'and Grand Street is not where you are to go to find him. I threw out a bait to see if you would snap at it, but I find you timid, and therefore advise you to drop the matter entirely.' I was quite willing to do so, and answered him to this effect; whereupon, with a side glance I did not understand but which made me more or less uneasy in regard to his intentions towards me, he motioned to the men who held my arms to let go their hold, which they at once did.

"'We have your signature,' growled the old man as I went out. 'If you peach on us or trouble us in any way we will show it to your father and that will put an end to all your hopes of future fortune.' Then raising his voice he shouted to the girl in the outer office, 'Let the young man see what he has signed.' She smiled and again brought forward the book in which I had so recklessly placed my name, and there at the top of the page I read these words: 'For moneys received, I agree to notify Levi Solomon, within the month, of the death of my father, that he may recover from me, without loss of time, the sum of ten thousand dollars from the amount I am bound to receive as my father's heir.' The sight of these lines knocked me hollow. But I am less of a coward morally than physically, and I determined to acquaint my father at once with what I had done, and get his advice as to whether or not I should inform the police of my adventure. He heard me with more consideration than I expected, but insisted that I should immediately make known to you my experience in this Bowery pawnbroker's shop.

"The officer, highly interested, took down the young man's statement in writing, and, after getting a more accurate description of the Jew's house, allowed his visitor to go.

"Fortunately for me I was in the building at the time, and was able to respond when a man was called up to investigate this matter. Thinking that I saw a connection between it and the various mysterious deaths of which I have previously spoken, I entered into the affair with much spirit. But, wishing to be sure that my possibly unwarranted conclusions were correct, I took pains to inquire, before proceeding upon my errand, into the character of the heirs who had inherited the property of Elwood Henderson and Christopher Bigelow, and found that in each case there was one among the rest who was well known for his profligacy and reckless expenditure. It was a significant discovery, and increased, if possible, my interest in running down this nefarious trafficker in the lives of wealthy men.

"Knowing that I could hope for no success in my character of detective, I made an arrangement with the father of the young gentleman before alluded to, by which I was to enter the pawn-shop as an emissary of the latter. I accordingly appeared there, one dull November afternoon, in the garb of a certain western sporting man, who, for a consideration, allowed me the temporary use of his name and credentials.

"Entering beneath the three golden balls, with, the swagger and general air of ownership I thought most likely to impose upon the self-satisfied female who presided over the desk, I asked to see her boss.

"'On your own business?' she queried, glancing with suspicion at my short coat, which was rather more showy than elegant.

"'No,' I returned, 'not on my own business, but on that of a young gent—'

"'Anyone whose name is written here?' she interposed, reaching towards me the famous book, over the top of which, however, she was careful to lay her arm.

"I glanced down the page she had opened and instantly detected that of the young gentleman on whose behalf I was supposed to be there, and nodded 'Yes,' with all the assurance of which I was capable.

"'Very well, then,' said she, 'come!' and she ushered me without much ado into a den of discomfort where sat a man, with a great beard and such heavy overhanging eyebrows that I could hardly detect the twinkle of his eyes, keen and incisive as they were.

"Smiling upon him, but not in the same way I had upon the girl, I glanced behind me at the open door, and above me at the partitions, which failed to reach the ceiling. Then I shook my head and drew a step nearer.

"'I have come,' I insinuatingly whispered, 'on behalf of a certain party who left this place in a huff a day or so ago, but who since then has had time to think the matter over, and has sent me with an apology which he hopes'—here I put on a diabolical smile, copied, I declare to you, from the one I saw at that moment on his own lips—'you will accept.'

"The old wretch regarded me for full two minutes in a way to unmask me had I possessed less confidence in my disguise and in my ability to support it.

"'And what is this young gentleman's name?' he finally asked.

"For reply, I handed him a slip of paper. He took it and read the few lines written on it, after which he began to rub his palms together with a snaky unction eminently in keeping with the stray glints of light that now and then found their way through his' bushy eyebrows.

"'And so the young gentleman had not the courage to come again himself?' he softly suggested, with just the suspicion of an ironical laugh. 'Thought, perhaps, I would exact too much commission; or make him pay too roundly for his impertinent assurance.'

"I shrugged my shoulders, but vouchsafed no immediate reply, and he saw that he had to open the business himself. He did it warily and with many an incisive question which would have tripped me up if I had not been very much on my guard; but it all ended, as such matters usually do, in mutual understanding, and a promise that if the young gentleman was willing to sign a certain paper, which, by the way, was not shown me, he would in exchange give him an address which, if made proper use of, would lead to my patron finding himself an independent man within a very few days.

"As this address was the thing above all others which I most desired, I professed myself satisfied with the arrangement, and proceeded to hunt up my patron, as he was called. Informing him of the result of my visit, I asked if his interest in ferreting out these criminals was strong enough to lead him to sign the vile document which the Jew would probably have in readiness for him on the morrow; and being told it was, we separated for that day, with the understanding that we were to meet the next morning at the spot chosen by the Jew for the completion of his nefarious bargain.

"Being certain that I was being followed in all my movements by the agents of this adept in villainy, I took care, upon leaving Mr. L—, to repair to the hotel of the sporting man I was personifying. Making myself square with the proprietor, I took up my quarters in the room of my sporting friend, and, the better to deceive any spy who might be lurking about, I received his letters and sent out his telegrams, which, if they did not create confusion in the affairs of 'The Plunger,' must at least have occasioned him no little work the next day.

"Promptly at ten o'clock on the following morning I met my patron at the place of rendezvous appointed by the old Jew; and when I tell you that this was no other than the old cemetery of which a portion is still to be seen off Chatham Square, you will understand the uncanny nature of this whole adventure, and the lurking sense there was in it of brooding death and horror. The scene, which in these days is disturbed by elevated railroad trains and the flapping of long lines of parti-colored clothes strung high up across the quiet tombstones, was at that time one of peaceful rest, in the midst of a quarter devoted to everything for which that rest is the fitting and desirable end; and as we paused among the mossy stones, we found it hard to realize that in a few minutes there would be standing beside us the concentrated essence of all that was evil and despicable in human nature.

"He arrived with a smile on his countenance that completed his ugliness, and would have frightened any honest man from his side at once. Merely glancing my way, he shuffled up to my companion, and leading him aside, drew out a paper which he laid on a flat tombstone with a gesture significant of his desire that the other should affix to it the required signature.

"Meantime I stood guard, and while attempting to whistle a light air, was carelessly taking in the surroundings, and conjecturing, as best I might, the reasons which had induced the old ghoul to make use of this spot for his diabolical business, and had about decided that it was because he was a ghoul, and thus felt at home among the symbols of mortality, when I caught sight of two or three young fellows, who were lounging on the other side of the fence.

"These were so evidently accomplices that I wondered if the two sly boys I had engaged to stand by me through this affair had spotted them, and would know enough to follow them back to their haunts.

"A few minutes later, the old rascal came sneaking towards me, with a gleam of satisfaction in his half-closed eyes.

"'You are not wanted any longer,' he grunted. 'The young gentleman told me to say that he could look out for himself now.'

"'The young gentleman had better pay me the round fifty he promised me,' I grumbled in return, with that sudden change from indifference to menace which I thought best calculated to further my plans; and shouldering the miserable wretch aside, I stepped up to my companion, who was still lingering in a state of hesitation among the gravestones.

"'Quick! Tell me the number and street which he has given you! ' I whispered, in a tone strangely in contrast with the angry and reproachful air I had assumed.

"He was about to answer, when the old fellow came sidling up behind us. Instantly the young man before me rose to the occasion, and putting on an air of conciliation said in a soothing tone:

"'There, there, don't bluster. Do one thing more for me, and I will add another fifty to those I promised you. Conjure up an anonymous letter—you know how—and send it to my father, saying that if he wants to know where his son loses his hundreds, he must go to the place on the dock, opposite 5 South Street, some night shortly after nine. It would not work with most men, but it will with my father, and when he has been in and out of that place, and I succeed to the fortune he will leave me, then I will remember you, and—'

"'Say, too,' a sinister voice here added in my ear, 'that if he wishes to effect an entrance into the gambling den which his son haunts, he must take the precaution of tying a bit of blue ribbon in his button-hole. It is a signal meaning business, and must not be forgotten,' chuckled the old fellow, evidently deceived at last into thinking I was really one of his own kind.

"I answered by a wink, and taking care to attempt no further communication with my patron, I left the two, as soon as possible, and went back to the hotel, where I dropped 'the sport,' and assumed a character and dress which enabled me to make my way undetected to the house of my young patron, where for two days I lay low, waiting for a suitable time in which to make my final attempt to penetrate this mystery.

"I knew that for the adventure I was now contemplating considerable courage was required. But I did not hesitate. The time had come for me to show my mettle. In the few communications I was enabled to hold with my superiors I told them of my progress and arranged with them my plan of work. As we all agreed that I was about to encounter no common villainy, these plans naturally partook of finesse, as you will see if you will follow my narrative to the end.

"Early in the evening of a cool November night I sallied forth into the streets, dressed in the habiliments and wearing the guise of the wealthy old gentleman whose secret guest I had been for the last few days. As he was old and portly, and I young and spare, this disguise had cost me no little thought and labor. But assisted as I was by the darkness, I had but little fear of betraying myself to any chance spy who might be upon the watch, especially as Mr. L— had a peculiar walk, which, in my short stay with him, I had learned to imitate perfectly. In the lapel of my overcoat I had tied a tag of blue ribbon, and, though for all I knew this was a signal devoting me to a secret and mysterious death, I walked along in a buoyant condition of mind, attributable, no doubt, to the excitement of the venture and to my desire to test my powers, even at the risk of my life.

"It was nine o'clock when I reached South Street. It was no new region to me, nor was I ignorant of the specified drinking den on the dock to which I had been directed. I remembered it as a bright spot in a mass of ship-prows and bow-rigging, and was possessed, besides, of a vague consciousness that there was something odd in connection with it which had aroused my curiosity sufficiently in the past for me to have once formed the resolution of seeing it again under circumstances which would allow me to give, it some attention. But I never thought that the circumstances would involve my own life, impossible as it is for a detective to reckon upon the future or to foresee the events into which he will be hurried by the next crime which may be reported at police headquarters.

"There were but few persons in the street when I crossed to The Heart's Delight,—so named from the heart-shaped opening in the framework of the door, through which shone a light, inviting enough to one chilled by the keen November air and oppressed by the desolate appearance of the almost deserted street. But amongst those persons I thought I recognized more than one familiar form, and felt reassured as to the watch which had been set upon the house. The night was dark and the river especially so, but in the gloomy space beyond the dock I detected a shadow blacker than the rest, which I took for the police-boat they had promised to have in readiness in case I needed rescue from the water-side. Otherwise the surroundings were as usual, and saving the gruff singing of some drunken sailor coming from a narrow side street nearby, no sound disturbed the somewhat lugubrious silence of this weird and forsaken spot.

"Pausing an instant before entering, I glanced up at the building, which was about three stories high, and endeavored to see what there was about it which had once arrested my attention, and came to the conclusion that it was its exceptional situation on the dock, and the ghostly effect of the hoisting-beam projecting from the upper story like a gibbet. And yet this beam was common to many a warehouse in the vicinity, though in none of them were there any such signs of life as proceeded from the curious mixture of sail loft, boat shop and drinking saloon, now before me. Could it be that the ban of criminality was upon the house, and that I had been conscious of this without being able to realize the cause of my interest?

"Not stopping to solve my sensations further, I tried the door, and, finding it yield easily to my touch, turned the knob and entered. For a moment I was blinded by the smoky glare of the heated atmosphere into which I stepped, but presently I was able to distinguish the vague outlines of an oyster bar in the distance, and the motionless figures of some half dozen men, whose movements had been arrested by my sudden entrance. For an instant this picture remained; then the drinking and card-playing were resumed, and I stood, as it were, alone on the sanded floor near the door. Improving the opportunity for a closer inspection of the place, I was struck by its picturesqueness. It had evidently been once used as a ship chandlery, and on the walls, which were but partly plastered, there still hung old bits of marlin, rusty rings and such other evidences of former traffic as did not interfere with the present more lucrative business.

"Below were the two bars, one at the right of the door, and the other at the lower end of the room near a window, through whose small, square panes I caught a glimpse of the colored lights of a couple of ferry boats, passing each other in midstream.

"At a table near me sat two men, grumbling at each other over a game of cards. They were large and powerful figures in the contracted space of this long and narrow room, and my heart gave a bound of joy as I recognized on them certain marks by which I was to know friend from foe in this possible den of thieves and murderers.

"Two sailors at the bar were bona fide habitués of the place, and so I judged to be the one or two other specimens of water-side character whose backs I could faintly discern in one of the dim corners. Meantime a man was approaching me.

"Let me see if I can describe him. He was about thirty, and had the complexion and figure of a consumptive, but his eye shone with the yellow glare of a beast of prey, and in the cadaverous hollows of his ashen cheeks and amid the lines about his thin drawn lips there lay for all his conciliatory smile, an expression so cold and yet so ferocious that I spotted him at once as the man to whose genius we were indebted for the new scheme of murder which I was jeopardizing my life to understand. But I allowed none of the repugnance with which he inspired me to appear in my manner, and, greeting him with half a nod, waited for him to speak. His voice had that smooth quality which betrays the hypocrite.

"'Has the gentleman an appointment here?' he asked, letting his glance fall for the merest instant on the lapel of my coat.

"I returned a decided affirmative. Or rather, I went on, with a meaning look he evidently comprehended, 'my son has, and I have made up my mind to know just what deviltry he is up to these days. You see I can make it worth your while to give me the opportunity.'

"'O, I see,' he assented with a glance at the pocketbook I had just drawn out. 'You want a private room from which you can watch the young scapegrace. I understand, I understand. But the private rooms are above. Gentlemen are not comfortable here.'

"'I should say not,' I murmured, and drew from the pocketbook a bill which I slid quietly into his hand. 'Now take me where I shall be safe,' I suggested, 'and yet in full sight of the room where the young gentlemen play. I wish to catch him at his tricks. Afterwards—'

"'All will be well,' he finished smoothly, with another glance at my blue ribbon. 'You see I do not ask you the young gentleman's name. I take your money and leave all the rest to you. Only don't make a scandal, I pray, for my house has the name of being quiet.'

"'Yes,' thought I, 'too quiet!' and for an instant felt my spirits fail me. But it was only for an instant. I had friends about me and a pistol at half cock in the pocket of my overcoat. Why should I fear any surprise, prepared as I was for every emergency?

"'I will show you up in a moment,' said he; and left me to put up a heavy board-shutter over the window opening on the river. Was this a signal or a precaution? I glanced towards my two friends playing cards, took another note of their broad shoulders and brawny arms, and prepared to follow my host, who now stood bowing at the other end of the room, before a covered staircase which was manifestly the sole means of reaching the floor above.

"The staircase was quite a feature in the room. It ran from back to front, and was boarded all the way up to the ceiling. On these boards hung a few useless bits of chain, wire and knotted ends of tarred ropes, which swung to and fro as the sharp November blast struck the building, giving out a weird and strangely muffled sound. Why did this sound, so easily to be accounted for, ring in my ears like a note of warning? I understand now, but I did not then, full of expectation as I was for developments out of the ordinary.

"Crossing the room, I entered upon the staircase, in the wake of my companion. Though the two men at cards did not look up as I passed them, I noticed that they were alert and ready for any signal I might choose to give them. But I was not ready to give one yet. I must see danger before I summoned help, and there was no token of danger yet.

"When we were about half-way up the stairs the faint light which had illuminated us from below suddenly vanished, and we found ourselves in total darkness. The door at the foot had been closed by a careful hand, and I felt, rather than heard, the stealthy pushing of a bolt across it.

"My first impulse was to forsake my guide and rush back, but I subdued the unworthy impulse and stood quite still, while my companion exclaiming, 'Damn that fellow! What does he mean by shutting the door before we're half-way up!' struck a match and lit a gas jet in the room above, which poured a flood of light upon the staircase. Drawing my hand from the pocket in which I had put my revolver, I hastened after him into the small landing at the top of the stairs. An open door was before me, in which he stood bowing, with the half-burnt match in his hand. 'This is the place, sir,' he announced, motioning me in.

"I entered and he remained by the door, while I passed quickly about the room, which was bare of every article of furniture save a solitary table and chair. There was not even a window in it, with the exception of one small light situated so high up in the corner made by the jutting-up staircase that I wondered at its use, and was only relieved of extreme apprehension at the prison-like appearance of the place by the gleam of light which came through this dusty pane, showing that I was not entirely removed from the presence of my foes if I was from that of my friends.

"'Ah, you have spied the window,' remarked my host, advancing toward me with a countenance he vainly endeavored to make reassuring and friendly. 'That is your post of observation, sir,' he whispered, with a great show of mystery. 'By mounting on the table you can peer into the room where my young friends sit securely at play.'

"As it was not part of my scheme to show any special mistrust, I merely smiled a little grimly, and cast a glance at the table on which stood a bottle of brandy and one glass.

"'Very good brandy,' he whispered, 'Not such stuff as we give those fellows down-stairs.'

"I shrugged my shoulders and he slowly backed towards the door.

"'The young men you bid me watch are very quiet,' I suggested, with a careless wave of my hand towards the room he had mentioned.

"'Oh, there is no one there yet. They begin to straggle in about ten o'clock.'

"'Ah,' was my quiet rejoinder, 'I am likely, then, to have use for your brandy.'

"He smiled again and made a swift motion towards the door.

"'If you want anything,' said he, 'just step to the foot of the staircase and let me know. The whole establishment is at your service.' And with one final grin that remains in my mind as the most threatening and diabolical I have ever witnessed, he laid his hand on the knob of the door and slid quickly out.

"It was done with such an air of final farewell, that I felt my apprehensions take a positive form. Rushing towards the door through which he had just vanished, I listened and heard, as I thought, his stealthy feet descend the stair. But when I sought to follow, I found myself for the second time overwhelmed by darkness. The gas jet, which had hitherto burned with great brightness in the small room, had been turned off from below, and beyond the faint glimmer which found its way through the small window of which I have spoken, not a ray of light now disturbed the heavy gloom of this gruesome apartment.

"I had thought of every contingency but this, and for a few minutes my spirits were dashed. But I soon recovered some remnants of self-possession, and began feeling for the knob I could no longer see. Finding it after a few futile attempts, I was relieved to discover that this door at least was not locked; and, opening it with a careful hand, I listened intently, but could hear nothing save the smothered sound of men talking in the room below.

"Should I signal for my companions? No, for the secret was not yet mine as to how men passed from this room into the watery grave which was the evident goal for all wearers of the blue ribbon.

"Stepping back into the middle of the room, I carefully pondered my situation, but could get no further than the fact that I was somehow, and in some way, in mortal peril. Would it come in the form of a bullet, or a deadly thrust from an unseen knife? I did not think so. For, to say nothing of the darkness, there was one reassuring fact which recurred constantly to my mind in connection with the murders I was endeavoring to trace to this den of iniquity.

"None of the gentlemen who had been found drowned had shown any marks of violence on their bodies, so it was not attack I was to fear, but some mysterious, underhanded treachery which would rob me of consciousness and make the precipitation of my body into the water both safe and easy. Perhaps it was in the bottle of brandy that the peril lay; perhaps—but why speculate further! I would watch till midnight and then, if nothing happened, signal my companions to raid the house.

"Meantime a peep into the next room might help me towards solving the mystery. Setting the bottle and glass aside, I dragged the table across the floor, placed it under the lighted window, mounted, and was about to peer through, when the light in that apartment was put out also. Angry and overwhelmed, I leapt down, and, stretching out my hands till they touched the wainscoting, I followed the wall around till I came to the knob of the door, which I frantically clutched. But I did not turn it immediately, I was too anxious to catch these villains at work. Would I be conscious of the harm they meditated against me, or would I imperceptibly yield to some influence of which I was not yet conscious, and drop to the floor before I could draw my revolver or put to my mouth the whistle upon which I de-pended for assistance and safety? It was hard to tell, but I determined to cling to my first intention a little longer, and so stood waiting and counting the minutes, while wondering if the captain of the police boat was not getting impatient, and whether I had not more to fear from the anxiety of my friends than the cupidity of my foes.

"You see I had anticipated communicating with the men in this boat by certain signals and tokens which had been arranged between us. But the lack of windows in the room had made all such arrangements futile, so I knew as little of their actions as they of my sufferings; all of which did not tend to add to the cheerfulness of my position.

"I, however, held out for a half-hour, listening, waiting and watching in a darkness which, like that of Egypt, could be felt, and when the suspense grew intolerable I struck a match and let its blue flame flicker for a moment over the face of my watch. But the matches soon gave out and with them my patience, if not my courage, and I determined to end the suspense by knocking at the door beneath.

"This resolution taken, I pulled open the door before me and stepped out. Though I could see nothing, I remembered the narrow landing at the top of the stairs, and, stretching out my arms, I felt for the boarding on either hand, guilding myself by it, and began to descend, when something rising, as it were, out of the cavernous darkness before me made me halt and draw back in mingled dread and horror.

"But the impression, strong as it was, was only momentary, and, resolved to be done with the matter, I precipitated myself downward, when suddenly, at about the middle of the staircase, my feet slipped and I slid forward, plunging and reaching out with hands whose frenzied grasp found nothing to cling to, down a steep inclined plane—or what to my bewildered senses appeared such,—till I struck a yielding surface and passed with one sickening plunge into the icy waters of the river which in another moment had closed dark and benumbing above my head.

"It was all so rapid I did not think of uttering a cry. But happily for me the splash I made told the story, and I was rescued before I could sink a second time.

"It was a full half hour before I had sufficiently recovered from the shock to relate my story. But when once I had made it known, you can imagine the gusto with which the police prepared to enter the house and confound the obliging host with a sight of my dripping garments and accusing face. And indeed in all my professional experience I have never beheld a more sudden merging of the bully into a coward than was to be seen in this slick villain's face, when I was suddenly pulled from the crowd and placed before him, with the old man's wig gone from my head, and the tag of blue ribbon still clinging to my wet coat.

"His game was up, and he saw it; and Ebenezer Gryce's career had begun.

"Like all destructive things the device by which I had been run into the river was simple enough when understood. In the first place it had been constructed to serve the purpose of a stairway and chute. The latter was in plain sight when it was used by the sailmakers to run the finished sails into the waiting yawls below. At the time of my adventure, and for some time before, the possibilities of the place had been discovered by mine host, who had ingeniously put a partition up the entire stairway, dividing the steps from the smooth runway. At the upper part of the runway he had built a few steps, wherewith to lure the unwary far enough down to insure a fatal descent. To make sure of his game he had likewise ceiled the upper room all around, including the enclosure of the stairs. The door to the chute and the door to the stairs were side by side, and being made of the same boards as the wainscoting, were scarcely visible when closed, while the single knob that was used, being transferable from one to the other, naturally gave the impression that there was but one door. When this adroit villain called my attention to the little window around the corner, he no doubt removed the knob from the stairs' door and quickly placed it in the one opening upon the chute. Another door, connecting the two similar landings without, explains how he got from the chute staircase into which he passed, on leaving me, to the one communicating with the room below.

"The mystery was solved, and my footing on the force secured; but to this day—and I am an old man now—I have not forgotten the horror of the moment when my feet slipped from under me, and I felt myself sliding downward, without hope of rescue, into a pit of heaving waters, where so many men of conspicuous virtue had already ended their valuable lives.

"Myriad thoughts flashed through my brain in that brief interval, and among them the whole method of operating this death-trap, together with every detail of evidence that would secure the conviction of the entire gang."

THE DOCTOR, HIS WIFE, AND THE CLOCK

I

On the 17th of July, 1851, a tragedy of no little interest occurred in one of the residences of the Colonnade in Lafayette Place.

Mr. Hasbrouck, a well-known and highly respected citizen, was attacked in his room by an unknown assailant, and shot dead before assistance could reach him. His murderer escaped, and the problem offered to the police was, how to identify this person who, by some happy chance or by the exercise of the most remarkable forethought, had left no traces behind him, or any clue by which he could be followed.

The affair was given to a young man, named Ebenezer Gryce, to investigate, and the story, as he tells it, is this:

When, some time after midnight, I reached Lafayette Place, I found the block lighted from end to end. Groups of excited men and women peered from the open doorways, and mingled their shadows with those of the huge pillars which adorn the front of this picturesque block of dwellings.

The house in which the crime had been committed was near the centre of the row, and, long before I reached it, I had learned from more than one source that the alarm was first given to the street by a woman's shriek, and secondly by the shouts of an old man-servant who had appeared, in a half-dressed condition, at the window of Mr. Hasbrouck's room, crying "Murder! murder!"

But when I had crossed the threshold, I was astonished at the paucity of the facts to be gleaned from the inmates themselves. The old servitor, who was the first to talk, had only this account of the crime to give.

The family, which consisted of Mr. Hasbrouck, his wife, and three servants, had retired for the night at the usual hour and under the usual auspices. At eleven o'clock the lights were all extinguished, and the whole household asleep, with the possible exception of Mr. Hasbrouck himself, who, being a man of large business responsibilities, was frequently troubled with insomnia.

Suddenly Mrs. Hasbrouck woke with a start. Had she dreamed the words that were ringing in her ears, or had they been actually uttered in her hearing? They were short, sharp words, full of terror and menace, and she had nearly satisfied herself that she had imagined them, when there came, from somewhere near the door, a sound she neither understood nor could interpret, but which filled her with inexplicable terror, and made her afraid to breathe, or even to stretch forth her hand towards her husband, whom she supposed to be sleeping at her side. At length another strange sound, which she was sure was not due to her imagination, drove her to make an attempt to rouse him, when she was horrified to find that she was alone in the bed, and her husband nowhere within reach.

Filled now with something more than nervous apprehension, she flung herself to the floor, and tried to penetrate, with frenzied glances, the surrounding darkness. But the blinds and shutters both having been carefully closed by Mr. Hasbrouck before retiring, she found this impossible, and she was about to sink in terror to the floor, when she heard a low gasp on the other side of the room, followed by the suppressed cry:

"God! what have I done!"

The voice was a strange one, but before the fear aroused by this fact could culminate in a shriek of dismay, she caught the sound of retreating footsteps, and, eagerly listening, she heard them descend the stairs and depart by the front door.

Had she known what had occurred—had there been no doubt in her mind as to what lay in the darkness on the other side of the room—it is likely that, at the noise caused by the closing front door, she would have made at once for the balcony that opened out from the window before which she was standing, and taken one look at the flying figure below. But her uncertainty as to what lay hidden from her by the darkness chained her feet to the floor, and there is no knowing when she would have moved, if a carriage had not at that moment passed down Astor Place, bringing with it a sense of companionship which broke the spell that held her, and gave her strength to light the gas, which was in ready reach of her hand.

As the sudden blaze illuminated the room, revealing in a burst the old familiar walls and well-known pieces of furniture, she felt for a moment as if released from some heavy nightmare and restored to the common experiences of life. But in another instant her former dread returned, and she found herself quaking at the prospect of passing around the foot of the bed into that part of the room which was as yet hidden from her eyes.

But the desperation which comes with great crises finally drove her from her retreat; and, creeping slowly forward, she cast one glance at the floor before her, when she found her worst fears realized by the sight of the dead body of her husband lying prone before the open doorway, with a bullet-hole in his forehead.

Her first impulse was to shriek, but, by a powerful exercise of will, she checked herself, and, ringing frantically for the servants who slept on the top-floor of the house, flew to the nearest window and endeavored to open it. But the shutters had been bolted so securely by Mr. Hasbrouck, in his endeavor to shut out light and sound, that by the time she had succeeded in unfastening them, all trace of the flying murderer had vanished from the street.

Sick with grief and terror, she stepped back into the room just as the three frightened servants descended the stairs. As they appeared in the open doorway, she pointed at her husband's inanimate form, and then, as if suddenly realizing in its full force the calamity which had befallen her, she threw up her arms, and sank forward to the floor in a dead faint.

The two women rushed to her assistance, but the old butler, bounding over the bed, sprang to the window, and shrieked his alarm to the street.

In the interim that followed, Mrs. Hasbrouck was revived, and the master's body laid decently on the bed; but no pursuit was made, nor any inquiries started likely to assist me in establishing the identity of the assailant.

Indeed, every one, both in the house and out, seemed dazed by the unexpected catastrophe, and as no one had any suspicions to offer as to the probable murderer, I had a difficult task before me.

I began, in the usual way, by inspecting the scene of the murder. I found nothing in the room, or in the condition of the body itself, which added an iota to the knowledge already obtained. That Mr. Hasbrouck had been in bed; that he had risen upon hearing a noise; and that he had been shot before reaching the door, were self-evident facts. But there was nothing to guide me further. The very simplicity of the circumstances caused a dearth of clues, which made the difficulty of procedure as great as any I ever encountered.

My search through the hall and down the stairs elicited nothing; and an investigation of the bolts and bars by which the house was secured, assured me that the assassin had either entered by the front door, or had already been secreted in the house when it was locked up for the night.

"I shall have to trouble Mrs. Hasbrouck for a short interview," I hereupon announced to the trembling old servitor, who had followed me like a dog about the house.

He made no demur, and in a few minutes I was ushered into the presence of the newly made widow, who sat quite alone, in a large chamber in the rear. As I crossed the threshold she looked up, and I encountered a good plain face, without the shadow of guile in it.

"Madam," said I, "I have not come to disturb you. I will ask two or three questions only, and then leave you to your grief. I am told that some words came from the assassin before he delivered his fatal shot. Did you hear these distinctly enough to tell me what they were?"

"I was sound asleep," said she, "and dreamt, as I thought, that a fierce, strange voice cried somewhere to some one: 'Ah! you did not expect me!' But I dare not say that these words were really uttered to my husband, for he was not the man to call forth hate, and only a man in the extremity of passion could address such an exclamation in such a tone as rings in my memory in connection with the fatal shot which woke me."

"But that shot was not the work of a friend," I argued. "If, as these words seem to prove, the assassin had some other motive than gain in his assault, then your husband had an enemy, though you never suspected it."

"Impossible!" was her steady reply, uttered in the most convincing tone. "The man who shot him was a common burglar, and, frightened at having been betrayed into murder, fled without looking for booty. I am sure I heard him cry out in terror and remorse: 'God! what have I done!'"

"Was that before you left the side of the bed?"

"Yes; I did not move from my place till I heard the front door close. I was paralyzed by my fear and dread."

"Are you in the habit of trusting to the security of a latch-lock only in the fastening of your front door at night? I am told that the big key was not in the lock, and that the bolt at the bottom of the door was not drawn."

"The bolt at the bottom of the door is never drawn. Mr. Hasbrouck was so good a man he never mistrusted any one. That is why the big lock was not fastened. The key, not working well, he took it some days ago to the locksmith, and when the latter failed to return it, he laughed, and said he thought no one would ever think of meddling with his front door."

"Is there more than one night-key to your house?" I now asked.

She shook her head.

"And when did Mr. Hasbrouck last use his?"

"To-night, when he came home from prayer-meeting," she answered, and burst into tears.

Her grief was so real and her loss so recent that I hesitated to afflict her by further questions. So returning to the scene of the tragedy, I stepped out upon the balcony which ran in front. Soft voices instantly struck my ears. The neighbors on either side were grouped in front of their own windows, and were exchanging the remarks natural under the circumstances. I paused, as in duty bound, and listened. But I heard nothing worth recording, and would have instantly re-entered the house, if I had not been impressed by the appearance of a very graceful woman who stood at my right. She was clinging to her husband, who was gazing at one of the pillars before him in a strange, fixed way which astonished me till he attempted to move, and then I saw that he was blind. Instantly I remembered that there lived in this row a blind doctor, equally celebrated for his skill and for his uncommon personal attractions, and, greatly interested not only in his affliction, but in the sympathy evinced for him by his young and affectionate wife, I stood still till I heard her say in the soft and appealing tones of love:

"Come in, Constant; you have heavy duties for to-morrow, and you should get a few hours' rest, if possible."

He came from the shadow of the pillar, and for one minute I saw his face with the lamplight shining full upon it. It was as regular of feature as a sculptured Adonis, and it was as white.

"Sleep!" he repeated, in the measured tones of deep but suppressed feeling. "Sleep! with murder on the other side of the wall!" And he stretched out his arms in a dazed way that insensibly accentuated the horror I myself felt of the crime which had so lately taken place in the room behind me.

She, noting the movement, took one of the groping hands in her own and drew him gently towards her.

"This way," she urged; and, guiding him into the house, she closed the window and drew down the shades, making the street seem darker by the loss of her exquisite presence.

This may seem a digression, but I was at the time a young man of thirty, and much under the dominion of woman's beauty. I was therefore slow in leaving the balcony, and persistent in my wish to learn something of this remarkable couple before leaving Mr. Hasbrouck's house.

The story told me was very simple. Dr. Zabriskie had not been born blind, but had become so after a grievous illness which had stricken him down soon after he received his diploma. Instead of succumbing to an affliction which would have daunted most men, he expressed his intention of practising his profession, and soon became so successful in it that he found no difficulty in establishing himself in one of the best-paying quarters of the city. Indeed, his intuition seemed to have developed in a remarkable degree after his loss of sight, and he seldom, if ever, made a mistake in diagnosis. Considering this fact, and the personal attractions which gave him distinction, it was no wonder that he soon became a popular physician whose presence was a benefaction and whose word a law.

He had been engaged to be married at the time of his illness, and, when he learned what was likely to be its results, had offered to release the young lady from all obligation to him. But she would not be released, and they were married. This had taken place some five years previous to Mr. Hasbrouck's death, three of which had been spent by them in Lafayette Place.

So much for the beautiful woman next door.

There being absolutely no clue to the assailant of Mr. Hasbrouck, I naturally looked forward to the inquest for some evidence upon which to work. But there seemed to be no underlying facts to this tragedy. The most careful study into the habits and conduct of the deceased brought nothing to light save his general beneficence and rectitude, nor was there in his history or in that of his wife any secret or hidden obligation calculated to provoke any such act of revenge as murder. Mrs. Hasbrouck's surmise that the intruder was simply a burglar, and that she had rather imagined than heard the words that pointed to the shooting as a deed of vengeance, soon gained general credence. But, though the police worked long and arduously in this new direction, their efforts were without fruit, and the case bade fair to remain an unsolvable mystery.

But the deeper the mystery the more persistently does my mind cling to it, and some five months after the matter had been delegated to oblivion, I found myself starting suddenly from sleep, with these words ringing in my ears:

"Who uttered the scream that gave the first alarm of Mr. Hasbrouck's violent death?"

I was in such a state of excitement that the perspiration stood out on my forehead. Mrs. Hasbrouck's story of the occurrence returned to me, and I remembered as distinctly as if she were then speaking, that she had expressly stated that she did not scream when confronted by the sight of her husband's dead body. But some one had screamed, and that very loudly. Who was it, then? One of the maids, startled by the sudden summons from below, or some one else—some involuntary witness of the crime, whose testimony had been suppressed at the inquest, by fear or influence?

The possibility of having come upon a clue even at this late day, so fired my ambition, that I took the first opportunity of revisiting Lafayette Place. Choosing such persons as I thought most open to my questions, I learned that there were many who could testify to having heard a woman's shrill scream on that memorable night just prior to the alarm given by old Cyrus, but no one who could tell from whose lips it had come. One fact, however, was immediately settled. It had not been the result of the servant-women's fears. Both of the girls were positive that they had uttered no sound, nor had they themselves heard any, till Cyrus rushed to the window with his wild cries. As the scream, by whomever given, was uttered before they descended the stairs, I was convinced by these assurances that it had issued from one of the front windows, and not from the rear of the house, where their own rooms lay. Could it be that it had sprung from the adjoining dwelling, and that— My thoughts went no further, but I made up my mind to visit the Doctor's house at once.

It took some courage to do this, for the Doctor's wife had attended the inquest, and her beauty, seen in broad daylight, had worn such an aspect of mingled sweetness and dignity, that I hesitated to encounter it under any circumstances likely to disturb its pure serenity. But a clue, once grasped, cannot be lightly set aside by a true detective, and it would have taken more than a woman's frown to stop me at this point. So I rang Dr. Zabriskie's bell.

I am seventy years old now and am no longer daunted by the charms of a beautiful woman, but I confess that when I found myself in the fine reception parlor on the first-floor, I experienced no little trepidation at the prospect of the interview which awaited me.

But as soon as the fine commanding form of the Doctor's wife crossed the threshold, I recovered my senses and surveyed her with as direct a gaze as my position allowed. For her aspect bespoke a degree of emotion that astonished me; and even before I spoke I perceived her to be trembling, though she was a woman of no little natural dignity and self-possession.

"I seem to know your face," she said, advancing courteously towards me, "but your name"—and here she glanced at the card she held in her hand—"is totally unfamiliar to me."

"I think you saw me some eighteen months ago," said I. "I am the detective who gave testimony at the inquest which was held over the remains of Mr. Hasbrouck."

I had not meant to startle her, but at this introduction of myself I saw her naturally pale cheek turn paler, and her fine eyes, which had been fixed curiously upon me, gradually sink to the floor.

"Great heaven!" thought I, "what is this I have stumbled upon!"

"I do not understand what business you can have with me," she presently remarked, with a show of gentle indifference that did not in the least deceive me.

"I do not wonder," I rejoined. "The crime which took place next door is almost forgotten by the community, and even if it were not, I am sure you would find it difficult to conjecture the nature of the question I have to put to you."

"I am surprised," she began, rising in her involuntary emotion and thereby compelling me to rise also. "How can you have any question to ask me on this subject? Yet if you have," she continued, with a rapid change of manner that touched my heart in spite of myself, "I shall, of course, do my best to answer you."

There are women whose sweetest tones and most charming smiles only serve to awaken distrust in men of my calling; but Mrs. Zabriskie was not of this number. Her face was beautiful, but it was also candid in its expression, and beneath the agitation which palpably disturbed her, I was sure there lurked nothing either wicked or false. Yet I held fast by the clue which I had grasped, as it were, in the dark, and without knowing whither I was tending, much less whither I was leading her, I proceeded to say:

"The question which I presume to put to you as the next-door neighbor of Mr. Hasbrouck, is this: Who was the woman who screamed out so loudly that the whole neighborhood heard her on the night of that gentleman's assassination?"

The gasp she gave answered my question in a way she little realized, and, struck as I was by the impalpable links that had led me to the threshold of this hitherto unsolvable mystery, I was about to press my advantage and ask another question, when she quickly started forward and laid her hand on my lips.

Astonished, I looked at her inquiringly, but her head was turned aside, and her eyes, fixed upon the door, showed the greatest anxiety. Instantly I realized what she feared. Her husband was entering the house, and she dreaded lest his ears should catch a word of our conversation.

Not knowing what was in her mind, and unable to realize the importance of the moment to her, I yet listened to the advance of her blind husband with an almost painful interest. Would he enter the room where we were, or would he pass immediately to his office in the rear? She seemed to wonder too, and almost held her breath as he neared the door, paused, and stood in the open doorway, with his ear turned towards us.

As for myself, I remained perfectly still, gazing at his face in mingled surprise and apprehension. For besides its beauty, which was of a marked order, as I have already observed, it had a touching expression which irresistibly aroused both pity and interest in the spectator. This may have been the result of his affliction, or it may have sprung from some deeper cause; but, whatever its source, this look in his face produced a strong impression upon me and interested me at once in his personality. Would he enter? Or would he pass on? Her look of silent appeal showed me in which direction her wishes lay, but while I answered her glance by complete silence, I was conscious in some indistinct way that the business I had undertaken would be better furthered by his entrance.

The blind have been often said to possess a sixth sense in place of the one they have lost. Though I am sure we made no noise, I soon perceived that he was aware of our presence. Stepping hastily forward he said, in the high and vibrating tone of restrained passion:

"Helen, are you here?"

For a moment I thought she did not mean to answer, but knowing doubtless from experience the impossibility of deceiving him, she answered with a cheerful assent, dropping her hand as she did so from before my lips.

He heard the slight rustle which accompanied the movement, and a look I found it hard to comprehend flashed over his features, altering his expression so completely that he seemed another man.

"You have some one with you," he declared, advancing another step but with none of the uncertainty which usually accompanies the movements of the blind. "Some dear friend," he went on, with an almost sarcastic emphasis and a forced smile that had little of gaiety in it.

The agitated and distressed blush which answered him could have but one interpretation. He suspected that her hand had been clasped in mine, and she perceived his thought and knew that I perceived it also.

Drawing herself up, she moved towards him, saying in a sweet womanly tone that to me spoke volumes:

never committed, and assured her that the matter would be inquired into very carefully before any attempt was made upon his liberty.

She thanked me, and, slowly rising, tried to regain her equanimity; but the manner as well as the matter of her husband's self-condemnation was too overwhelming in its nature for her to recover readily from her emotions.

"I have long dreaded this," she acknowledged. "For months I have foreseen that he would make some rash communication or insane avowal. If I had dared, I would have consulted some physician about this hallucination of his; but he was so sane on other points that I hesitated to give my dreadful secret to the world. I kept hoping that time and his daily pursuits would have their effect and restore him to himself. But his illusion grows, and now I fear that nothing will ever convince him that he did not commit the deed of which he accuses himself. If he were not blind I would have more hope, but the blind have so much time for brooding."

"I think he had better be indulged in his fancies for the present," I ventured. "If he is laboring under an illusion it might be dangerous to cross him."

"If?" she echoed in an indescribable tone of amazement and dread. "Can you for a moment harbor the idea that he has spoken the truth?"

"Madam," I returned, with something of the cynicism of my later years, "what caused you to give such an unearthly scream just before this murder was made known to the neighborhood?"

She stared, paled, and finally began to tremble, not, as I now believe, at the insinuation latent in my words, but at the doubts which my question aroused in her own breast.

"Did I?" she asked; then with a great burst of candor, which seemed inseparable from her nature, she continued: "Why do I try to mislead you or deceive myself? I did give a shriek just before the alarm was raised next door; but it was not from any knowledge I had of a crime having been committed, but because I unexpectedly saw before me my husband whom I supposed to be on his way to Poughkeepsie. He was looking very pale and strange, and for a moment I thought I was beholding his ghost. But he soon explained his appearance by saying that he had fallen from the train and had been only saved by a miracle from being dismembered; and I was just bemoaning his mishap and trying to calm him and myself, when that terrible shout was heard next door of 'Murder! murder!' Coming so soon after the shock he had himself experienced, it quite unnerved him, and I think we can date his mental disturbance from that moment. For he began almost immediately to take a morbid interest in the affair next door, though it was weeks, if not months, before he let a word fall of the nature of those you have just heard. Indeed it was not till I repeated to him some of the expressions he was continually letting fall in his sleep, that he commenced to accuse himself of crime and talk of retribution."

"You say that your husband frightened you on that night by appearing suddenly at the door when you thought him on his way to Poughkeepsie. Is Dr. Zabriskie in the habit of thus going and coming alone at an hour so late as this must have been?"

"You forget that to the blind, night is less full of perils than the day. Often and often has my husband found his way to his patients' houses alone after midnight; but on this especial evening he had Harry with him. Harry was his driver, and always accompanied him when he went any distance."

"Well, then," said I, "all we have to do is to summon Harry and hear what he has to say concerning this affair. He surely will know whether or not his master went into the house next door."

"Harry has left us," she said. "Dr. Zabriskie has another driver now. Besides—(I have nothing to conceal from you)—Harry was not with him when he returned to the house that evening, or the Doctor would not have been without his portmanteau till the next day. Something—I have never known what—caused them to separate, and that is why I have no answer to give the Doctor when he accuses himself of committing a deed on that night which is wholly out of keeping with every other act of his life."

"And have you never questioned Harry why they separated and why he allowed his master to come home alone after the shock he had received at the station?"

"I did not know there was any reason for doing so till long after he left us."

"And when did he leave?"

"That I do not remember. A few weeks or possibly a few days after that dreadful night."

"And where is he now?"

"Ah, that I have not the least means of knowing. But," she suddenly cried, "what do you want of Harry? If he did not follow Dr. Zabriskie to his own door, he could tell us nothing that would convince my husband that he is laboring under an illusion."

"But he might tell us something which would convince us that Dr. Zabriskie was not himself after the accident, that he—"

"Hush!" came from her lips in imperious tones. "I will not believe that he shot Mr. Hasbrouck even if you prove him to have been insane at the time. How could he? My husband is blind. It would take a man of very keen sight to force himself into a house that was closed for the night, and kill a man in the dark at one shot."

"Rather," cried a voice from the doorway, "it is only a blind man who could do this. Those who trust to eyesight must be able to catch some glimpse of the mark they aim at, and this room, as I have been told, was without a glimmer of light. But the blind trust to sound, and as Mr. Hasbrouck spoke—"

"Oh!" burst from the horrified wife, "is there no one to stop him when he speaks like that?"

II

When I related to my superiors the details of the foregoing interview, two of them coincided with the wife in thinking that Dr. Zabriskie was in an irresponsible condition of mind which made any statement of his questionable. But the third seemed disposed to argue the matter, and, casting me an inquiring look, seemed to ask what my opinion was on the subject. Answering him as if he had spoken, I gave my conclusion as follows: That whether insane or not, Dr. Zabriskie had fired the shot which terminated Mr. Hasbrouck's life.

It was the Inspector's own idea, but it was not shared in by the others, one of whom had known the Doctor for years. Accordingly they compromised by postponing all opinion till they had themselves interrogated the Doctor, and I was detailed to bring him before them the next afternoon.

He came without reluctance, his wife accompanying him. In the short time which elapsed between their leaving Lafayette Place and entering Headquarters, I embraced the opportunity of observing them, and I found the study equally exciting and interesting. His face was calm but hopeless, and his eye, which should have shown a wild glimmer if there was truth in his wife's hypothesis, was dark and unfathomable, but neither frenzied nor uncertain. He spake but once and listened to nothing, though now and then his wife moved as if to attract his attention, and once even stole her hand toward his, in the tender hope that he would feel its approach and accept her sympathy. But he was deaf as well as blind; and sat wrapped up in thoughts which she, I know, would have given worlds to penetrate.

Her countenance was not without its mystery also. She showed in every lineament passionate concern and misery, and a deep tenderness from which the element of fear was not absent. But she, as well as he, betrayed that some misunderstanding, deeper than any I had previously suspected, drew its intangible veil between them and made the near proximity in which they sat, at once a heart-piercing delight and an unspeakable pain. What was this misunderstanding? and what was the character of the fear that modified her every look of love in his direction? Her perfect indifference to my presence proved that it was not connected with the position in which he had put himself towards the police by his voluntary confession of crime, nor could I thus interpret the expression of frantic question which now and then contracted her features, as she raised her eyes towards his sightless orbs, and strove to read, in his firm-set lips, the meaning of those assertions she could only ascribe to a loss of reason.

The stopping of the carriage seemed to awaken both from thoughts that separated rather than united them. He turned his face in her direction, and she, stretching forth her hand, prepared to lead him from the carriage, without any of that display of timidity which had been previously evident in her manner.

As his guide she seemed to fear nothing; as his lover, everything.

"There is another and a deeper tragedy underlying the outward and obvious one," was my inward conclusion, as I followed them into the presence of the gentlemen awaiting them.

Dr. Zabriskie's appearance was a shock to those who knew him; so was his manner, which was calm, straightforward, and quietly determined.

"I shot Mr. Hasbrouck," was his steady affirmation, given without any show of frenzy or desperation. "If you ask me why I did it, I cannot answer; if you ask me how, I am ready to state all that I know concerning the matter."

"But, Dr. Zabriskie," interposed his friend, "the why is the most important thing for us to consider just now. If you really desire to convince us that you committed the dreadful crime of killing a totally inoffensive man, you should give us some reason for an act so opposed to all your instincts and general conduct."

But the Doctor continued unmoved:

"I had no reason for murdering Mr. Hasbrouck. A hundred questions can elicit no other reply; you had better keep to the how."

A deep-drawn breath from the wife answered the looks of the three gentlemen to whom this suggestion was offered. "You see," that breath seemed to protest, "that he is not in his right mind."

I began to waver in my own opinion, and yet the intuition which has served me in cases as seemingly impenetrable as this, bade me beware of following the general judgment.

"Ask him to inform you how he got into the house," I whispered to Inspector D—, who sat nearest me.

Immediately the Inspector put the question I had suggested:

"By what means did you enter Mr. Hasbrouck's house at so late an hour as this murder occurred?"

The blind doctor's head fell forward on his breast, and he hesitated for the first and only time.

"You will not believe me," said he; "but the door was ajar when I came to it. Such things make crime easy; it is the only excuse I have to offer for this dreadful deed."

The front door of a respectable citizen's house ajar at half-past eleven at night. It was a statement that fixed in all minds the conviction of the speaker's irresponsibility. Mrs. Zabriskie's brow cleared, and her beauty became for a moment dazzling as she held out her hands in irrepressible relief towards those who were interrogating her husband. I alone kept my impassibility. A possible explanation of this crime had flashed like lightning across my mind; an explanation from which I inwardly recoiled, even while I was forced to consider it.

"Dr. Zabriskie," remarked the Inspector who was most friendly to him, "such old servants as those kept by Mr. Hasbrouck do not leave the front door ajar at twelve o'clock at night."

"Yet ajar it was," repeated the blind doctor, with quiet emphasis; "and finding it so, I went in. When I came out again, I closed it. Do you wish me to swear to what I say? If so, I am ready."

What could we reply? To see this splendid-looking man, hallowed by an affliction so great that in itself it called forth the compassion of the most indifferent, accusing himself of a cold-blooded crime, in tones that sounded dispassionate because of the will that forced their utterance, was too painful in itself for us to indulge in any unnecessary words. Compassion took the place of curiosity, and each and all of us turned involuntary looks of pity upon the young wife pressing so eagerly to his side.

"For a blind man," ventured one, "the assault was both deft and certain. Are you accustomed to Mr. Hasbrouck's house, that you found your way with so little difficulty to his bedroom?"

"I am accustomed—" he began.

But here his wife broke in with irrepressible passion:

"He is not accustomed to that house. He has never been beyond the first-floor. Why, why do you question him? Do you not see—"

His hand was on her lips.

"Hush!" he commanded. "You know my skill in moving about a house; how I sometimes deceive those who do not know me into believing that I can see, by the readiness with which I avoid obstacles and find my way even in strange and untried scenes. Do not try to make them think I am not in my right mind, or you will drive me into the very condition you deprecate."

His face, rigid, cold, and set, looked like that of a mask. Hers, drawn with horror and filled with question that was fast taking the form of doubt, bespoke an awful tragedy from which more that one of us recoiled.

"Can you shoot a man dead without seeing him?" asked the Superintendent, with painful effort.

"Give me a pistol and I will show you," was the quick reply.

A low cry came from the wife. In a drawer near to every one of us there lay a pistol, but no one moved to take it out. There was a look in the Doctor's eye which made us fear to trust him with a pistol just then.

"We will accept your assurance that you possess a skill beyond that of most men," returned the Superintendent. And beckoning me forward, he whispered: "This is a case for the doctors and not for the police. Remove him quietly, and notify Dr. Southyard of what I say."

But Dr. Zabriskie, who seemed to have an almost supernatural acuteness of hearing, gave a violent start at this and spoke up for the first time with real passion in his voice:

"No, no, I pray you. I can bear anything but that. Remember, gentlemen, that I am blind; that I cannot see who is about me; that my life would be a torture if I felt myself surrounded by spies watching to catch some evidence of madness in me. Rather conviction at once, death, dishonor, and obloquy. These I have incurred. These I have brought upon myself by crime, but not this worse fate—oh! not this worse fate."

His passion was so intense and yet so confined within the bounds of decorum, that we felt strangely impressed by it. Only the wife stood transfixed, with the dread growing in her heart, till her white, waxen visage seemed even more terrible to contemplate than his passion-distorted one.

"It is not strange that my wife thinks me demented," the Doctor continued, as if afraid of the silence that answered him. "But it is your business to discriminate, and you should know a sane man when you see him."

Inspector D— no longer hesitated.

"Very well," said he, "give us the least proof that your assertions are true, and we will lay your case before the prosecuting attorney."

"Proof? Is not a man's word—"

"No man's confession is worth much without some evidence to support it. In your case there is none. You cannot even produce the pistol with which you assert yourself to have committed the deed."

"True, true. I was frightened by what I had done, and the instinct of self-preservation led me to rid myself of the weapon in any way I could. But some one found this pistol; some one picked it up from the sidewalk of Lafayette Place on that fatal night. Advertise for it. Offer a reward. I will give you the money." Suddenly he appeared to realize how all this sounded. "Alas!" cried he, "I know the story seems improbable; all I say seems improbable; but it is not the probable things that happen in this life, but the improbable, as you should know, who every day dig deep into the heart of human affairs."

Were these the ravings of insanity? I began to understand the wife's terror.

"I bought the pistol," he went on, "of—alas! I cannot tell you his name. Everything is against me. I cannot adduce one proof; yet she, even she, is beginning to fear that my story is true. I know it by her silence, a silence that yawns between us like a deep and unfathomable gulf."

But at these words her voice rang out with passionate vehemence.

"No, no, it is false! I will never believe that your hands have been plunged in blood. You are my own pure-hearted Constant, cold, perhaps, and stern, but with no guilt upon your conscience, save in your own wild imagination."

"Helen, you are no friend to me," he declared, pushing her gently aside. "Believe me innocent, but say nothing to lead these others to doubt my word."

And she said no more, but her looks spoke volumes.

The result was that he was not detained, though he prayed for instant commitment. He seemed to dread his own home, and the surveillance to which he instinctively knew he would henceforth be subjected. To see him shrink from his wife's hand as she strove to lead him from the room was sufficiently painful; but the feeling thus aroused was nothing to that with which we observed the keen and agonized expectancy of his look as he turned and listened for the steps of the officer who followed him.

"I shall never again know whether or not I am alone," was his final observation as he left our presence.

I said nothing to my superiors of the thoughts I had had while listening to the above interrogatories. A theory had presented itself to my mind which explained in some measure the mysteries of the Doctor's conduct, but I wished for time and opportunity to test its reasonableness before submitting it to their higher judgment. And these seemed likely to be given me, for the Inspectors continued divided in their opinion of the blind physician's guilt, and the District-Attorney, when told of the affair, pooh-poohed it without mercy, and declined to stir in the matter unless some tangible evidence were forthcoming to substantiate the poor Doctor's self-accusations.

"If guilty, why does he shrink from giving his motives," said he, "and if so anxious to go to the gallows, why does he suppress the very facts calculated to send him there? He is as mad as a March hare, and it is to an asylum he should go and not to a jail."

In this conclusion I failed to agree with him, and as time wore on my suspicions took shape and finally ended in a fixed conviction. Dr. Zabriskie had committed the crime he avowed, but—let me proceed a little further with my story before I reveal what lies beyond that "but."

Notwithstanding Dr. Zabriskie's almost frenzied appeal for solitude, a man had been placed in surveillance over him in the shape of a young doctor skilled in diseases of the brain. This man communicated more or less with the police, and one morning I received from him the following extracts from the diary he had been ordered to keep.

"The Doctor is settling into a deep melancholy from which he tries to rise at times, but with only indifferent success. Yesterday he rode around to all his patients for the purpose of withdrawing his services on the plea of illness. But he still keeps his office open, and to-day I had the opportunity of witnessing his reception and treatment of the many sufferers who came to him for aid. I think he was conscious of my presence, though an attempt had been made to conceal it. For the listening look never left his face from the moment he entered the room, and once he rose and passed quickly from wall to wall, groping with outstretched hands into every nook and corner, and barely escaping contact with the curtain behind which I was hidden. But if he suspected my presence, he showed no displeasure at it, wishing perhaps for a witness to his skill in the treatment of disease.

"And truly I never beheld a finer manifestation of practical insight in cases of a more or less baffling nature than I beheld in him to-day. He is certainly a most wonderful physician, and I feel bound to record that his mind is as clear for business as if no shadow had fallen upon it.

"Dr. Zabriskie loves his wife, but in a way that tortures both himself and her. If she is gone from the house he is wretched, and yet when she returns he often forbears to speak to her, or if he does speak, it is with a constraint that hurts her more than his silence. I was present when she came in to-day. Her step, which had been eager on the stairway, flagged as she approached the room, and he naturally noted the change and gave his own interpretation to it. His face, which had been very pale, flushed suddenly, and a nervous trembling seized him which he sought in vain to hide. But by the time her tall and beautiful figure stood in the doorway he was his usual self again in all but the expression of his eyes, which stared straight before him in an agony of longing only to be observed in those who have once seen.

"'Where have you been, Helen?' he asked, as, contrary to his wont, he moved to meet her.

"'To my mother's, to Arnold & Constable's, and to the hospital, as you requested,' was her quick answer, made without faltering or embarrassment.

"He stepped still nearer and took her hand, and as he did so my physician's eye noted how his finger lay over her pulse in seeming unconsciousness.

"'Nowhere else?' he queried.

"She smiled the saddest kind of smile and shook her head; then, remembering that he could not see this movement, she cried in a wistful tone:

"'Nowhere else, Constant; I was too anxious to get back.'

"I expected him to drop her hand at this, but he did not; and his finger still rested on her pulse.

"'And whom did you see while you were gone?' he continued.

"She told him, naming over several names.

"'You must have enjoyed yourself,' was his cold comment, as he let go her hand and turned away. But his manner showed relief, and I could not but sympathize with the pitiable situation of a man who found himself forced to means like these for probing the heart of his young wife.

"Yet when I turned towards her I realized that her position was but little happier than his. Tears are no strangers to her eyes, but those that welled up at this moment seemed to possess a bitterness that promised but little peace for her future. Yet she quickly dried them and busied herself with ministrations for his comfort.

"If I am any judge of woman, Helen Zabriskie is superior to most of her sex. That her husband mistrusts her is evident, but whether this is the result of the stand she has taken in his regard, or only a manifestation of dementia, I have as yet been unable to determine. I dread to leave them alone together, and yet when I presume to suggest that she should be on her guard in her interviews with him, she smiles very placidly and tells me that nothing would give her greater joy than to see him lift his hand against her, for that would argue that he is not accountable for his deeds or for his assertions.

"Yet it would be a grief to see her injured by this passionate and unhappy man.

"You have said that you wanted all details I could give; so I feel bound to say, that Dr. Zabriskie tries to be considerate of his wife, though he often fails in the attempt. When she offers herself as his guide, or assists him with his mail, or performs any of the many acts of kindness by which she continually manifests her sense of his affliction, he thanks her with courtesy and often with kindness, yet I know she would willingly exchange all his set phrases for one fond embrace or impulsive smile of affection. That he is not in the full possession of his faculties would be too much to say, and yet upon what other hypothesis can we account for the inconsistencies of his conduct.

"I have before me two visions of mental suffering. At noon I passed the office door, and looking within, saw the figure of Dr. Zabriskie seated in his great chair, lost in thought or deep in those memories which make an abyss in one's consciousness. His hands, which were clenched, rested upon the arms of his chair, and in one of them I detected a woman's glove, which I had no difficulty in recognizing as one of the pair worn by his wife this morning. He held it as a tiger might hold his prey or a miser his gold, but his set features and sightless eyes betrayed that a conflict of emotions was waging within him, among which tenderness had but little share.

"Though alive, as he usually is, to every sound, he was too absorbed at this moment to notice my presence though I had taken no pains to approach quietly. I therefore stood for a full minute watching him, till an irresistible sense of the shame of thus spying upon a blind man in his moments of secret anguish seized upon me and I turned away. But not before I saw his features relax in a storm of passionate feeling, as he rained kisses after kisses on the senseless kid he had so long held in his motionless grasp. Yet when an hour later he entered the dining-room on his wife's arm, there was nothing in his manner to show that he had in any way changed in his attitude towards her.

"The other picture was more tragic still. I have no business with Mrs. Zabriskie's affairs; but as I passed upstairs to my room an hour ago, I caught a fleeting vision of her tall form, with the arms thrown up over her head in a paroxysm of feeling which made her as oblivious to my presence as her husband had been several hours before. Were the words that escaped her lips 'Thank God we have no children!' or was this exclamation suggested to me by the passion and unrestrained impulse of her action?"

Side by side with these lines, I, Ebenezer Gryce, placed the following extracts from my own diary:

"Watched the Zabriskie mansion for five hours this morning, from the second story window of an adjoining hotel. Saw the Doctor when he drove away on his round of visits, and saw him when he returned. A colored man accompanied him.

"To-day I followed Mrs. Zabriskie. I had a motive for this, the nature of which I think it wisest not to divulge. She went first to a house in Washington Place where I am told her mother lives. Here she stayed some time, after which she drove down to Canal Street, where she did some shopping, and later stopped at the hospital, into which I took the liberty of following her. She seemed to know many there, and passed from cot to cot with a smile in which I alone discerned the sadness of a broken heart. When she left, I left also, without having learned anything beyond the fact that Mrs. Zabriskie is one who does her duty in sorrow as in happiness. A rare and trustworthy woman I should say, and yet her husband does not trust her. Why?

"I have spent this day in accumulating details in regard to Dr. and Mrs. Zabriskie's life previous to the death of Mr. Hasbrouck. I learned from sources it would be unwise to quote just here, that Mrs. Zabriskie had not lacked enemies ready to charge her with coquetry; that while she had never sacrificed her dignity in public, more than one person had been heard to declare, that Dr. Zabriskie was fortunate in being blind, since the sight of his wife's beauty would have but poorly compensated him for the pain he would have suffered in seeing how that beauty was admired.

"That all gossip is more or less tinged with exaggeration I have no doubt, yet when a name is mentioned in connection with such stories, there is usually some truth at the bottom of them. And a name is mentioned in this case, though I do not think it worth my while to repeat it here; and loth as I am to recognize the fact, it is a name that carries with it doubts that might easily account for the husband's jealousy. True, I have found no one who dares to hint that she still continues to attract attention or to bestow smiles in any direction save where they legally belong. For since a certain memorable night which we all know, neither Dr. Zabriskie nor his wife have been seen save in their own domestic circle, and it is not into such scenes that this serpent, of which I have spoken, ever intrudes, nor is it in places of sorrow or suffering that his smile shines, or his fascinations flourish.

"And so one portion of my theory is proved to be sound. Dr. Zabriskie is jealous of his wife: whether with good cause or bad I am not prepared to decide; for her present attitude, clouded as it is by the tragedy in which she and her husband are both involved, must differ very much from that which she held when her life was unshadowed by doubt, and her admirers could be counted by the score.

"I have just found out where Harry is. As he is in service some miles up the river, I shall have to be absent from my post for several hours, but I consider the game well worth the candle.

"Light at last. I have seen Harry, and, by means known only to the police, have succeeded in making him talk. His story is substantially this: That on the night so often mentioned, he packed his master's portmanteau at eight o'clock and at ten called a carriage and rode with the Doctor to the Twenty-ninth Street station. He was told to buy tickets for Poughkeepsie where his master had been called in consultation, and having done this, hurried back to join his master on the platform. They had walked together as far as the cars, and Dr. Zabriskie was just stepping on to the train when a man pushed himself hurriedly between them and whispered something into his master's ear, which caused him to fall back and lose his footing. Dr. Zabriskie's body slid half under the car, but he was withdrawn before any harm was done, though the cars gave a lurch at that moment which must have frightened him exceedingly, for his face was white when he rose to his feet, and when Harry offered to assist him again on to the train, he refused to go and said he would return home and not attempt to ride to Poughkeepsie that night.

"The gentleman, whom Harry now saw to be Mr. Stanton, an intimate friend of Dr. Zabriskie, smiled very queerly at this, and taking the Doctor's arm led him away to a carriage. Harry naturally followed them, but the Doctor, hearing his steps, turned and bade him, in a very peremptory tone, to take the omnibus home, and then, as if on second thought, told him to go to Poughkeepsie in his stead and explain to the people there that he was too shaken up by his mis-step to do his duty, and that he would be with them next morning. This seemed strange to Harry, but he had no reasons for disobeying his master's orders, and so rode to Poughkeepsie. But the Doctor did not follow him the next day; on the contrary he telegraphed for him to return, and when he got back dismissed him with a month's wages. This ended Harry's connection with the Zabriskie family.

"A simple story bearing out what the wife has already told us; but it furnishes a link which may prove invaluable. Mr. Stanton, whose first name is Theodore, knows the real reason why Dr. Zabriskie returned home on the night of the seventeenth of July, 1851. Mr. Stanton, consequently, I must see, and this shall be my business to-morrow.

"Checkmate! Theodore Stanton is not in this country. Though this points him out as the man from whom Dr. Zabriskie bought the pistol, it does not facilitate my work, which is becoming more and more difficult.

"Mr. Stanton's whereabouts are not even known to his most intimate friends. He sailed from this country most unexpectedly on the eighteenth of July a year ago, which was the day after the murder of Mr. Hasbrouck. It looks like a flight, especially as he has failed to maintain open communication even with his relatives. Was he the man who shot Mr. Hasbrouck? No; but he was the man who put the pistol in Dr. Zabriskie's hand that night, and, whether he did this with purpose or not, was evidently so alarmed at the catastrophe which followed that he took the first outgoing steamer to Europe. So far, all is clear, but there are mysteries yet to be solved, which will require my utmost tact. What if I should seek out the gentleman with whose name that of Mrs. Zabriskie has been linked, and see if I can in any way connect him with Mr. Stanton or the events of that night?

"Eureka! I have discovered that Mr. Stanton cherished a mortal hatred for the gentleman above mentioned. It was a covert feeling, but no less deadly on that account; and while it never led him into any extravagances, it was of force sufficient to account for many a secret misfortune which happened to that gentleman. Now, if I can prove he was the Mephistopheles who whispered insinuations into the ear of our blind Faust, I may strike a fact that will lead me out of this maze.

"But how can I approach secrets so delicate without compromising the woman I feel bound to respect, if only for the devoted love she manifests for her unhappy husband!

"I shall have to appeal to Joe Smithers. This is something which I always hate to do, but as long as he will take money, and as long as he is fertile in resources for obtaining the truth from people I am myself unable to reach, so long must I make use of his cupidity and his genius. He is an honorable fellow in one way, and never retails as gossip what he acquires for our use. How will he proceed in this case, and by what tactics will he gain the very delicate information which we need? I own that I am curious to see.

"I shall really have to put down at length the incidents of this night. I always knew that Joe Smithers was invaluable to the police, but I really did not know he possessed talents of so high an order. He wrote me this morning that he had succeeded in getting Mr. T—'s promise to spend the evening with him, and advised me that if I desired to be present also, his own servant would not be at home, and that an opener of bottles would be required.

"As I was very anxious to see Mr. T— with my own eyes, I accepted the invitation to play the spy upon a spy, and went at the proper hour to Mr. Smithers's rooms, which are in the University Building. I found them picturesque in the extreme. Piles of books stacked here and there to the ceiling made nooks and corners which could be quite shut off by a couple of old pictures that were set into movable frames that swung out or in at the whim or convenience of the owner.

"As I liked the dark shadows cast by these pictures, I pulled them both out, and made such other arrangements as appeared likely to facilitate the purpose I had in view, then I sat down and waited for the two gentlemen who were expected to come in together.

"They arrived almost immediately, whereupon I rose and played my part with all necessary discretion. While ridding Mr. T— of his overcoat, I stole a look at his face. It is not a handsome one, but it boasts of a gay, devil-may-care expression which doubtless makes it dangerous to many women, while his manners are especially attractive, and his voice the richest and most persuasive that I ever heard. I contrasted him, almost against my will, with Dr. Zabriskie, and decided that with most women the former's undoubted fascinations of speech and bearing would outweigh the latter's great beauty and mental endowments; but I doubted if they would with her.

"The conversation which immediately began was brilliant but desultory, for Mr. Smithers, with an airy lightness for which he is remarkable, introduced topic after topic, perhaps for the purpose of showing off Mr. T—'s versatility, and perhaps for the deeper and more sinister purpose of shaking the kaleidoscope of talk so thoroughly, that the real topic which we were met to discuss should not make an undue impression on the mind of his guest.

"Meanwhile one, two, three bottles passed, and I saw Joe Smithers's eye grow calmer and that of Mr. T— more brilliant and more uncertain. As the last bottle showed signs of failing, Joe cast me a meaning glance, and the real business of the evening began.

"I shall not attempt to relate the half-dozen failures which Joe made in endeavoring to elicit the facts we were in search of, without arousing the suspicion of his visitor. I am only going to relate the successful attempt. They had been talking now for some hours, and I, who had long before been waved from their immediate presence, was hiding my curiosity and growing excitement behind one of the pictures, when suddenly I heard Joe say:

"'He has the most remarkable memory I ever met. He can tell to a day when any notable event occurred.'

"'Pshaw!' answered his companion, who, by the by, was known to pride himself upon his own memory for dates, 'I can state where I went and what I did on every day in the year. That may not embrace what you call 'notable events,' but the memory required is all the more remarkable, is it not?'

"'Pooh!' was his friend's provoking reply, 'you are bluffing, Ben; I will never believe that.'

"Mr. T—, who had passed by this time into that state of intoxication which makes persistence in an assertion a duty as well as a pleasure, threw back his head, and as the wreaths of smoke rose in airy spirals from his lips, reiterated his statement, and offered to submit to any test of his vaunted powers which the other might dictate.

"'You have a diary—' began Joe.

"'Which is at home,' completed the other.

"'Will you allow me to refer to it to-morrow, if I am suspicious of the accuracy of your recollections?'

"'Undoubtedly,' returned the other.

"'Very well, then, I will wager you a cool fifty, that you cannot tell where you were between the hours of ten and eleven on a certain night which I will name.'

"'Done!' cried the other, bringing out his pocket-book and laying it on the table before him.

"Joe followed his example and then summoned me.

"'Write a date down here,' he commanded, pushing a piece of paper towards me, with a look keen as the flash of a blade. 'Any date, man,' he added, as I appeared to hesitate in the embarrassment I thought natural under the circumstances. 'Put down day, month, and year, only don't go too far back; not farther than two years.'

"Smiling with the air of a flunkey admitted to the sports of his superiors, I wrote a line and laid it before Mr. Smithers, who at once pushed it with a careless gesture towards his companion. You can of course guess the date I made use of: July 17, 1851. Mr. T—, who had evidently looked upon this matter as mere play, flushed scarlet as he read these words, and for one instant looked as if he had rather flee our presence than answer Joe Smithers's nonchalant glance of inquiry.

"'I have given my word and will keep it,' he said at last, but with a look in my direction that sent me reluctantly back to my retreat. 'I don't suppose you want names,' he went on, 'that is, if anything I have to tell is of a delicate nature?'

"'O no,' answered the other, 'only facts and places.'

"'I don't think places are necessary either,' he returned. 'I will tell you what I did and that must serve you. I did not promise to give number and street.'

"'Well, well,' Joe exclaimed; 'earn your fifty, that is all. Show that you remember where you were on the night of'—and with an admirable show of indifference he pretended to consult the paper between them—'the seventeenth of July, 1851, and I shall be satisfied.'

"'I was at the club for one thing,' said Mr. T—; 'then I went to see a lady friend, where I stayed till eleven. She wore a blue muslin— What is that?'

"I had betrayed myself by a quick movement which sent a glass tumbler crashing to the floor. Helen Zabriskie had worn a blue muslin on that same night. I had noted it when I stood on the balcony watching her and her husband.

"'That noise?' It was Joe who was speaking. 'You don't know Reuben as well as I do or you wouldn't ask. It is his practice, I am sorry to say, to accentuate his pleasure in draining my bottles, by dropping a glass at every third one.'

"Mr. T— went on.

"'She was a married woman and I thought she loved me; but—and this is the greatest proof I can offer you that I am giving you a true account of that night—she had not had the slightest idea of the extent of my passion, and only consented to see me at all because she thought, poor thing, that a word from her would set me straight, and rid her of attentions that were fast becoming obnoxious. A sorry figure for a fellow to cut who has not been without his triumphs; but you caught me on the most detestable date in my calendar, and—'

"There is where he stopped being interesting, so I will not waste time by quoting further. And now what reply shall I make when Joe Smithers asks me double his usual price, as he will be sure to do, next time? Has he not earned an advance? I really think so.

"I have spent the whole day in weaving together the facts I have gleaned, and the suspicions I have formed, into a consecutive whole likely to present my theory in a favorable light to my superiors. But just as I thought myself in shape to meet their inquiries, I received an immediate summons into their presence, where I was given a duty to perform of so extraordinary and unexpected a nature, that it effectually drove from my mind all my own plans for the elucidation of the Zabriskie mystery.

"This was nothing more nor less than to take charge of a party of people who were going to the Jersey heights for the purpose of testing Dr. Zabriskie's skill with a pistol."

III

The cause of this sudden move was soon explained to me. Mrs. Zabriskie, anxious to have an end put to the present condition of affairs, had begged for a more rigid examination into her husband's state. This being accorded, a strict and impartial inquiry had taken place, with a result not unlike that which followed the first one. Three out of his four interrogators judged him insane, and could not be moved from their opinion though opposed by the verdict of the young expert who had been living in the house with him. Dr. Zabriskie seemed to read their thoughts, and, showing extreme agitation, begged as before for an opportunity to prove his sanity by showing his skill in shooting. This time a disposition was evinced to grant his request, which Mrs. Zabriskie no sooner perceived, than she added her supplications to his that the question might be thus settled.

A pistol was accordingly brought; but at sight of it her courage failed, and she changed her prayer to an entreaty that the experiment should be postponed till the next day, and should then take place in the woods away from the sight and hearing of needless spectators.

Though it would have been much wiser to have ended the matter there and then, the Superintendent was prevailed upon to listen to her entreaties, and thus it was that I came to be a spectator, if not a participator, in the final scene of this most sombre drama.

There are some events which impress the human mind so deeply that their memory mingles with all after-experiences. Though I have made it a rule to forget as soon as possible the tragic episodes into which I am constantly plunged, there is one scene in my life which will not depart at my will; and that is the sight which met my eyes from the bow of the small boat in which Dr. Zabriskie and his wife were rowed over to Jersey on that memorable afternoon.

Though it was by no means late in the day, the sun was already sinking, and the bright red glare which filled the heavens and shone full upon the faces of the half-dozen persons before me added much to the tragic nature of the scene, though we were far from comprehending its full significance.

The Doctor sat with his wife in the stern, and it was upon their faces my glance was fixed. The glare shone luridly on his sightless eyeballs, and as I noticed his unwinking lids I realized as never before what it was to be blind in the midst of sunshine. Her eyes, on the contrary, were lowered, but there was a look of hopeless misery in her colorless face which made her appearance infinitely pathetic, and I felt confident that if he could only have seen her, he would not have maintained the cold and unresponsive manner which chilled the words on her lips and made all advance on her part impossible.

On the seat in front of them sat the Inspector and a doctor, and from some quarter, possibly from under the Inspector's coat, there came the monotonous ticking of a small clock, which, I had been told, was to serve as a target for the blind man's aim.

This ticking was all I heard, though the noise and bustle of a great traffic was pressing upon us on every side. And I am sure it was all that she heard, as, with hand pressed to her heart and eyes fixed on the opposite shore, she waited for the event which was to determine whether the man she loved was a criminal or only a being afflicted of God, and worthy of her unceasing care and devotion.

As the sun cast its last scarlet gleam over the water, the boat grounded, and it fell to my lot to assist Mrs. Zabriskie up the bank. As I did so, I allowed myself to say: "I am your friend, Mrs. Zabriskie," and was astonished to see her tremble, and turn toward me with a look like that of a frightened child.

But there was always this characteristic blending in her countenance of the childlike and the severe, such as may so often be seen in the faces of nuns, and beyond an added pang of pity for this beautiful but afflicted woman, I let the moment pass without giving it the weight it perhaps demanded.

"The Doctor and his wife had a long talk last night," was whispered in my ear as we wound our way along into the woods. I turned and perceived at my side the expert physician, portions of whose diary I have already quoted. He had come by another boat.

"But it did not seem to heal whatever breach lies between them," he proceeded. Then in a quick, curious tone, he asked: "Do you believe this attempt on his part is likely to prove anything but a farce?"

"I believe he will shatter the clock to pieces with his first shot," I answered, and could say no more, for we had already reached the ground which had been selected for this trial at arms, and the various members of the party were being placed in their several positions.

The Doctor, to whom light and darkness were alike, stood with his face towards the western glow, and at his side were grouped the Inspector and the two physicians. On the arm of one of the latter hung Dr. Zabriskie's overcoat, which he had taken off as soon as he reached the field.

Mrs. Zabriskie stood at the other end of the opening, near a tall stump, upon which it had been decided that the clock should be placed when the moment came for the Doctor to show his skill. She had been accorded the privilege of setting the clock on this stump, and I saw it shining in her hand as she paused for a moment to glance back at the circle of gentlemen who were awaiting her movements. The hands of the clock stood at five minutes to five, though I scarcely noted the fact at the time, for her eyes were on mine, and as she passed me she spoke:

"If he is not himself, he cannot be trusted. Watch him carefully, and see that he does no mischief to himself or others. Be at his right hand, and stop him if he does not handle his pistol properly."

I promised, and she passed on, setting the clock upon the stump and immediately drawing back to a suitable distance at the right, where she stood, wrapped in her long dark cloak, quite alone. Her face shone ghastly white, even in its environment of snow-covered boughs which surrounded her, and, noting this, I wished the minutes fewer between the present moment and the hour of five, at which he was to draw the trigger.

"Dr. Zabriskie," quoth the Inspector, "we have endeavored to make this trial a perfectly fair one. You are to have one shot at a small clock which has been placed within a suitable distance, and which you are expected to hit, guided only by the sound which it will make in striking the hour of five. Are you satisfied with the arrangement?"

"Perfectly. Where is my wife?"

"On the other side of the field, some ten paces from the stump upon which the clock is fixed."

He bowed, and his face showed satisfaction.

"May I expect the clock to strike soon?"

"In less than five minutes," was the answer.

"Then let me have the pistol; I wish to become acquainted with its size and weight."

We glanced at each other, then across at her.

She made a gesture; it was one of acquiescence.

Immediately the Inspector placed the weapon in the blind man's hand. It was at once apparent that the Doctor understood the instrument, and my last doubt vanished as to the truth of all he had told us.

"Thank God I am blind this hour and cannot see her," fell unconsciously from his lips; then, before the echo of these words had left my ears, he raised his voice and observed calmly enough, considering that he was about to prove himself a criminal in order to save himself from being thought a madman.

"Let no one move. I must have my ears free for catching the first stroke of the clock." And he raised the pistol before him.

There was a moment of torturing suspense and deep, unbroken silence. My eyes were on him, and so I did not watch the clock, but suddenly I was moved by some irresistible impulse to note how Mrs. Zabriskie was bearing herself at this critical moment, and, casting a hurried glance in her direction, I perceived her tall figure swaying from side to side, as if under an intolerable strain of feeling. Her eyes were on the clock, the hands of which seemed to creep with snail-like pace along the dial, when unexpectedly, and a full minute before the minute hand had reached the stroke of five, I caught a movement on her part, saw the flash of something round and white show for an instant against the darkness of her cloak, and was about to shriek warning to the Doctor, when the shrill, quick stroke of a clock rung out on the frosty air, followed by the ping and flash of a pistol.

A sound of shattered glass, followed by a suppressed cry, told us that the bullet had struck the mark, but before we could move, or rid our eyes of the smoke which the wind had blown into our faces, there came another sound which made our hair stand on end and sent the blood back in terror to our hearts. Another clock was striking, the clock which we now perceived was still standing upright on the stump where Mrs. Zabriskie had placed it.

Whence came the clock, then, which had struck before the time and been shattered for its pains? One quick look told us. On the ground, ten paces at the right, lay Helen Zabriskie, a broken clock at her side, and in her breast a bullet which was fast sapping the life from her sweet eyes.

We had to tell him, there was such pleading in her looks; and never shall I forget the scream that rang from his lips as he realized the truth. Breaking from our midst, he rushed forward, and fell at her feet as if guided by some supernatural instinct.

"Helen," he shrieked, "what is this? Were not my hands dyed deep enough in blood that you should make me answerable for your life also?"

Her eyes were closed, but she opened them. Looking long and steadily at his agonized face, she faltered forth:

"It is not you who have killed me; it is your crime. Had you been innocent of Mr. Hasbrouck's death, your bullet would never have found my heart. Did you think I could survive the proof that you had killed that good man?"

"I—I did it unwittingly. I—"

"Hush!" she commanded, with an awful look, which, happily, he could not see. "I had another motive. I wished to prove to you, even at the cost of my life, that I loved you, had always loved you, and not—"

It was now his turn to silence her. His hand crept over her lips, and his despairing face turned itself blindly towards us.

"Go," he cried; "leave us! Let me take a last farewell of my dying wife, without listeners or spectators."

Consulting the eye of the physician who stood beside me, and seeing no hope in it, I fell slowly back. The others followed, and the Doctor was left alone with his wife. From the distant position we took, we saw her arms creep round his neck, saw her head fall confidingly on his breast, then silence settled upon them and upon all nature, the gathering twilight deepening, till the last glow disappeared from the heavens above and from the circle of leafless trees which enclosed this tragedy from the outside world.

But at last there came a stir, and Dr. Zabriskie, rising up before us, with the dead body of his wife held closely to his breast, confronted us with a countenance so rapturous that he looked like a man transfigured.

"I will carry her to the boat," said he. "Not another hand shall touch her. She was my true wife, my true wife!" And he towered into an attitude of such dignity and passion, that for a moment he took on heroic proportions and we forgot that he had just proved himself to have committed a cold-blooded and ghastly crime.

The stars were shining when we again took our seats in the boat; and if the scene of our crossing to Jersey was impressive, what shall be said of that of our return.

The Doctor, as before, sat in the stern, an awesome figure, upon which the moon shone with a white radiance that seemed to lift his face out of the surrounding darkness and set it, like an image of frozen horror, before our eyes. Against his breast he held the form of his dead wife, and now and then I saw him stoop as if he were listening for some tokens of life at her set lips. Then he would lift himself again, with hopelessness stamped upon his features, only to lean forward in renewed hope that was again destined to disappointment.

The Inspector and the accompanying physician had taken seats in the bow, and unto me had been assigned the special duty of watching over the Doctor. This I did from a low seat in front of him. I was therefore so close that I heard his laboring breath, and though my heart was full of awe and compassion, I could not prevent myself from bending towards him and saying these words:

"Dr. Zabriskie, the mystery of your crime is no longer a mystery to me. Listen and see if I do not understand your temptation, and how you, a conscientious and God-fearing man, came to slay your innocent neighbor.

"A friend of yours, or so he called himself, had for a long time filled your ears with tales tending to make you suspicious of your wife and jealous of a certain man whom I will not name. You knew that your friend had a grudge against this man, and so for many months turned a deaf ear to his insinuations. But finally some change which you detected in your wife's bearing or conversation roused your own suspicions, and you began to doubt if all was false that came to your ears, and to curse your blindness, which in a measure rendered you helpless. The jealous fever grew and had risen to a high point, when one night—a memorable night—this friend met you just as you were leaving town, and with cruel craft whispered in your ear that the man you hated was even then with your wife, and that if you would return at once to your home you would find him in her company.

"The demon that lurks at the heart of all men, good or bad, thereupon took complete possession of you, and you answered this false friend by saying that you would not return without a pistol. Whereupon he offered to take you to his house and give you his. You consented, and getting rid of your servant by sending him to Poughkeepsie with your excuses, you entered a coach with your friend.

"You say you bought the pistol, and perhaps you did, but, however that may be, you left his house with it in your pocket and, declining companionship, walked home, arriving at the Colonnade a little before midnight.

"Ordinarily you have no difficulty in recognizing your own doorstep. But, being in a heated frame of mind, you walked faster than usual and so passed your own house and stopped at that of Mr. Hasbrouck's, one door beyond. As the entrances of these houses are all alike, there was but one way by which you could have made yourself sure that you had reached your own dwelling, and that was by feeling for the doctor's sign at the side of the door. But you never thought of that. Absorbed in dreams of vengeance, your sole impulse was to enter by the quickest means possible. Taking out your night-key, you thrust it into the lock. It fitted, but it took strength to turn it, so much strength that the key was twisted and bent by the effort. But this incident, which would have attracted your attention at another time, was lost upon you at this moment. An entrance had been effected, and you were in too excited a frame of mind to notice at what cost, or to detect the small differences apparent in the atmosphere and furnishings of the two houses—trifles which would have arrested your attention under other circumstances, and made you pause before the upper floor had been reached.

"It was while going up the stairs that you took out your pistol, so that by the time you arrived at the front-room door you held it ready cocked and drawn in your hand. For, being blind, you feared escape on the part of your victim, and so waited for nothing but the sound of a man's voice before firing. When, therefore, the unfortunate Mr. Hasbrouck, roused by this sudden intrusion, advanced with an exclamation of astonishment, you pulled the trigger, killing him on the spot. It must have been immediately upon his fall that you recognized from some word he uttered, or from some contact you may have had with your surroundings, that you were in the wrong house and had killed the wrong man; for you cried out, in evident remorse, 'God! what have I done!' and fled without approaching your victim.

"Descending the stairs, you rushed from the house, closing the front door behind you and regaining your own without being seen. But here you found yourself baffled in your attempted escape, by two things. First, by the pistol you still held in your hand, and secondly, by the fact that the key upon which you depended for entering your own door was so twisted out of shape that you knew it would be useless for you to attempt to use it. What did you do in this emergency? You have already told us, though the story seemed so improbable at the time, you found nobody to believe it but myself. The pistol you flung far away from you down the pavement, from which, by one of those rare chances which sometimes happen in this world, it was presently picked up by some late passer-by of more or less doubtful character. The door offered less of an obstacle than you anticipated; for when you turned to it again you found it, if I am not greatly mistaken, ajar, left so, as we have reason to believe, by one who had gone out of it but a few minutes before in a state which left him but little master of his actions. It was this fact which provided you with an answer when you were asked how you succeeded in getting into Mr. Hasbrouck's house after the family had retired for the night.

"Astonished at the coincidence, but hailing with gladness the deliverance which it offered, you went in and ascended at once into your wife's presence; and it was from her lips, and not from those of Mrs. Hasbrouck, that the cry arose which startled the neighborhood and prepared men's minds for the tragic words which were shouted a moment later from the next house.

"But she who uttered the scream knew of no tragedy save that which was taking place in her own breast. She had just repulsed a dastardly suitor, and, seeing you enter so unexpectedly in a state of unaccountable horror and agitation, was naturally stricken with dismay, and thought she saw your ghost, or, what was worse, a possible avenger; while you, having failed to kill the man you sought, and having killed a man you esteemed, let no surprise on her part lure you into any dangerous self-betrayal. You strove instead to soothe her, and even attempted to explain the excitement under which you labored, by an account of your narrow escape at the station, till the sudden alarm from next door distracted her attention, and sent both your thoughts and hers in a different direction. Not till conscience had fully awakened and the horror of your act had had time to tell upon your sensitive nature, did you breathe forth those vague confessions, which, not being supported by the only explanations which would have made them credible, led her, as well as the police, to consider you affected in your mind. Your pride as a man, and your consideration for her as a woman, kept you silent, but did not keep the worm from preying upon your heart.

"Am I not correct in my surmises, Dr. Zabriskie, and is not this the true explanation of your crime?"

With a strange look, he lifted up his face.

"Hush!" said he; "you will awaken her. See how peacefully she sleeps! I should not like to have her awakened now, she is so tired, and I—I have not watched over her as I should."

Appalled at his gesture, his look, his tone, I drew back, and for a few minutes no sound was to be heard but the steady dip-dip of the oars and the lap-lap of the waters against the boat. Then there came a quick uprising, the swaying before me of something dark and tall and threatening, and before I could speak or move, or even stretch forth my hands to stay him, the seat before me was empty and darkness had filled the place where but an instant previous he had sat, a fearsome figure, erect and rigid as a sphinx.

What little moonlight there was only served to show us a few rising bubbles, marking the spot where the unfortunate man had sunk with his much-loved burden. We could not save him. As the widening circles fled farther and farther out, the tide drifted us away, and we lost the spot which had seen the termination of one of earth's saddest tragedies.

The bodies were never recovered. The police reserved to themselves the right of withholding from the public the real facts which made this catastrophe an awful remembrance to those who witnessed it. A verdict of accidental death by drowning answered all purposes, and saved the memory of the unfortunate pair from such calumny as might have otherwise assailed it. It was the least we could do for two beings whom circumstances had so greatly afflicted.

X. Y. Z. A DETECTIVE STORY

CHAPTER I

THE MYSTERIOUS RENDEZVOUS

Sometimes in the course of his experience, a detective, while engaged in ferreting out the mystery of one crime, runs inadvertently upon the clue to another. But rarely has this been done in a manner more unexpected or with attendant circumstances of greater interest than in the instance I am now about to relate.

For some time the penetration of certain Washington officials had been baffled by the clever devices of a gang of counterfeiters who had inundated the western portion of Massachusetts with spurious Treasury notes. Some of the best talent of the Secret Service had been expended upon the matter, but with no favorable result, when, one day, notice was received at Washington that a number of suspicious-looking letters, addressed to the simple initials, X. Y. Z., Brandon, Mass., were being daily forwarded through the mails of that region; and it being deemed possible that a clue had at last been offered to the mystery in hand, I was sent northward to investigate.

It was in the middle of June, 1881, and the weather was simply delightful. As I stepped from the cars at Brandon and looked up the long straight street with its double row of maple trees sparkling fresh and beautiful in the noonday sun, I thought I had never seen a prettier village or entered upon any enterprise with a lighter or more hopeful heart.

Intent on my task, I went straight to the post-office, and after coming to an understanding with the postmaster, proceeded at once to look over the mail addressed to the mysterious X. Y. Z.

I found it to consist entirely of letters. They were about a dozen in number, and were, with one exception, similar in general appearance and manner of direction, though inscribed in widely different handwritings, and posted from various New England towns. The exception to which I allude had these few extra words written in the lower left-hand corner of the envelope: "To be kept till called for." As I bundled up the letters preparatory to thrusting them back into the box, I noticed that the latter was the only one in a blue envelope, all the others being in the various shades of cream-color and buff.

"Who is in the habit of calling for these letters?" I asked of the postmaster.

"Well," said he, "I don't know his name. The fact is nobody knows him around here. He usually drives up in a buggy about nightfall, calls for letters addressed to X. Y. Z., and having got them, whips up his horse and is off again before one can say a word."

"Describe him," said I.

"Well, he is very lean and very lank. In appearance he is both green and awkward. His complexion is pale, almost sickly. Were it not for his eye, which is keen and twinkling, I should call him an extremely inoffensive-looking person."

The type was not new to me. "I should like to see him," said I.

"You will have to wait till nightfall, then," returned the postmaster. "He never comes till about dusk. Drop in here, say at seven o'clock, and I will see that you have the opportunity of handing him his mail."

I nodded acquiescence to this and sauntered out of the enclosure devoted to the uses of the post-office. As I did so I ran against a young man who was hurriedly approaching from the other end of the store.

"Your pardon," he cried; and I turned to look at him, so gentlemanly was his tone, and so easy the bow with which he accompanied this simple apology.

He was standing before the window of the post-office, waiting for his mail; a good-looking, well-made young man, of a fine countenance, but with a restless eye, whose alert yet anxious expression I could not but note even in the casual glance I gave him. There appeared to be some difficulty in procuring him his mail, and each minute he was kept waiting seemed to increase his impatience almost beyond the bounds of endurance. I saw him lean forward and gasp out a hurried word to the postmaster, and was idly wondering over his anxiety and its probable causes, when I heard a hasty exclamation near me, and looking around, saw the postmaster himself beckoning to me from the door of the enclosure. I immediately hastened forward.

"I don't know what it means," he whispered; "but here is a young man, different from any who have been here before, asking for a letter addressed to X. Y. Z."

"A letter?" I repeated.

"Yes, a letter."

"Give him the whole batch and see what he does," I returned, drawing back where I could myself watch the result of my instructions. The postmaster did as I requested. In another moment I saw the young man start with amazement as a dozen letters were put in his hand. "These are not all for me!" he cried, but even as he made the exclamation, drew to one side, and with a look of mingled perplexity and concern, began opening them one after another, his expression deepening to amazement as he glanced at their contents. The one in the blue envelope, however, seemed to awaken quite different emotions. With an unconscious look of relief, he hastily read the short letter it contained, then with a quick gesture, folded it up and thrust it back into the envelope he held, together with the other letters, in his left hand.

"There must be another X. Y. Z.," said he, approaching the window of the post-office and handing back all the letters he had received, with the exception of the one in the blue envelope, which with a quick movement he had separated from the rest and thrust into his coat-pocket. "I can lay claim to none of these." And with a repetition of his easy bow he turned away and hurriedly quitted the store, followed by the eyes of clerks and customers, to whom he was evidently as much of a stranger as he was to me. Without hesitation I went to the door and looked after him. He was just crossing the street to the tavern on the other side of the way. I saw him enter, felt that he was safe to remain there for a few minutes, and conscious of the great opportunity awaiting me, hastened back to the postmaster.

"Well," cried I, in secret exultation, "our plan has worked admirably. Let me see the letters. As they have been opened, and through no fault of ours, a peep at them now in the cause of justice will harm none but the guilty."

The postmaster demurred, but I soon overcame his scruples; and taking down the letters once more, hastily investigated their contents. I own that I was considerably disappointed at the result. In fact, I found nothing that pointed toward the counterfeiters; only in each letter a written address, together with fifty cents' worth of stamps.

"Some common fraud," I exclaimed. "One of those cheap affairs where, for fifty cents enclosed, a piece of information calculated to insure fortune to the recipient is promised by return of mail."

And disgusted with the whole affair I bundled up the letters, and was about to replace them in the box for the third time when I discovered that it still held a folded paper. Drawing this out, I opened it and started in fresh amazement. If I was not very much mistaken in the appearance of the letter in the blue envelope which I had seen the young man read with so much interest, this was certainly it. But how came it here? Had I not seen him thrust it back into its envelope and afterward put envelope and all into his pocket? But here was no envelope, and here was the letter. By what freak of necromancy had it been transferred from its legitimate quarters to this spot? I could not imagine. Suddenly I remembered that his hand had been full of the other letters when he put, or endeavored to put, this special one back into its envelope, and however unaccountable it may seem, it must be that from haste or agitation he had only succeeded in thrusting it between two letters instead of into the envelope, as he supposed. Whether or not this explanation be true, there was no doubt about my luck being in the ascendant. Mastering my satisfaction, I read these lines written in what appeared to be a disguised hand.

"All goes well. The time has come; every thing is in train, and success is certain. Be in the shrubbery at the northeast corner of the grounds at 9 P.M. precisely; you will be given a mask and such other means as are necessary to insure you the accomplishment of the end you have in view. He cannot hold out against a surprise. The word, by which you will know your friends, is COUNTERFEIT."

"Ah, ha!" thought I, "this is more like it." And moved by a sudden impulse, I hastily copied the letter into my memorandum-book, and then returning to the original, scratched out with my penknife the word northeast and carefully substituting that of southwest put the letter back into the box, in the hope that when he came to consult the envelope in his pocket (as he would be sure to do sooner or later) he would miss its contents and return to the post-office in search of it.

Nor was I mistaken. I had scarcely accomplished my task, when he reëntered the store, asked to see the letters he had returned, and finding amongst them the one he had lost, disappeared with it back to the tavern. "If he is surprised to read southwest this time instead of northeast, he will think his memory played him false in the first instance," cried I, in inward comment over my last doubtful stroke of policy; and turning to the postmaster, I asked him what place there was in the vicinity which could be said to possess grounds and a shrubbery.

"There is but one," he returned, "Mr. Benson's. All the rest of the folks are too poor to indulge in any such gimcracks."

"And who is Mr. Benson?"

"Well, he is Mr. Benson, the richest man in these parts and the least liked as I take it. He came here from Boston two years ago and built a house fit for a king to live in. Why, nobody knows, for he seems to take no pleasure in it. His children do though, and that is all he cares for I suppose. Young Mr. Benson especially seems to be never tired of walking about the grounds, looking at the trees and tying up the vines. Miss Carrie is different; all she wants is company. But little of that has her father ever allowed her till this very day. He seems to think nobody is good enough to sit down in his parlors; and yet he don't sit there himself, the strange man! but is always shut up in his library or some other out-of-the-way place."

"A busy man?"

"I suppose so, but no one ever sees any thing he does."

"Writes, perhaps?"

"I don't know; he never talks about himself."

"How did he get his money?"

"That we don't know. It seems to accumulate without his help or interference. When he came here he was called rich, but to-day he is said to be worth three times what he was then."

"Perhaps he speculates?"

"If he does, it must be through his son, for he never leaves home himself."

"Has two children, you say?"

"Yes, a son and a daughter: a famous young man, the son; not so much liked, perhaps, as universally respected. He is too severe and reticent to be a favorite, but no one ever found him doing any thing unworthy of himself. He is the pride of the county, and if he were a bit suaver in manner might have been in Congress at this minute."

"How old?"

"Thirty, I should say."

"And the girl?"

"Twenty-five, perhaps."

"A mother living?"

"No; there were some strange stories of her having died a year or so before they came here, under circumstances of a somewhat distressing nature, but they themselves say nothing about it."

"It seems to me they don't say much about any thing."

"That's just it; they are the most reserved people you ever saw. It isn't from them we have heard there is another son floating somewhere about the world. They never speak of him, and what's more, they never write to him; as who should know better than myself?"

An interruption here occurred, and I took the opportunity to saunter out into the crowd of idlers always to be found hanging around a country store at mail-time. My purpose was, as you may conceive, to pick up any stray bits of information that might be floating about concerning these Bensons. Not that I had as yet discovered any thing definite connecting this respectable family with the gang of counterfeiters upon whose track I had been placed; but business is business, and no clue, however slight or unpromising in its nature, is to be neglected when the way is as dark as that which lay before me. With an easy smile, therefore, calculated to allay apprehension and awaken confidence, I took my stand among these loungers. But I soon found that I need do nothing to start the wheel of gossip on the subject of the Bensons. It was already going, and that with a force and spirit that almost took my breath away.

"A fancy ball!" were the first words I heard. "The Bensons give a fancy ball, when they never had three persons at a time in their house before!"

"Yes, and what's more, they are going to have folks over from Clayton and Lawrence and Hollowell and devil knows where. It's to be a smash up, a regular fandango, with masks and all that kind of nonsense."

"They say Miss Carrie teased her father till he had to give in in self-defence. It's her birthday or something like that, and she would have a party."

"But such a party! who ever heard the like in a respectable town like this! It's wicked, that's what I call it, downright wicked to cover up the face God has given you and go strutting around in clothes a Christian man might well think borrowed from the Evil One if he had to wear them in any decent company. All wrong, I say, all wrong, and I am astonished at Mr. Benson. To keep his doors shut as he has, and then to open them in a burst to all sorts of folly. We are not invited at our house."

"Nor we, nor we," shouted some half dozen.

"And I don't know of any one in this town who is," cried a burly man, presumably a butcher by trade. "We are not good enough for the Bensons. They say he is even going to be mean enough to shut the gates and not let a soul inside who hasn't a ticket. And they are going to light up the grounds too!"

"We can peep through the fence."

"Much we will see that way. If you had said climb it—"

"We can't climb it. Big John is going to be there and Tom Henshaw. They mean to keep their good times to themselves, just as they have kept every thing else. It's a queer set they are anyway, and the less we have to do with them the better."

"I should like to see Hartley Benson in masquerade costume, I would."

"Oh, he won't wear any of the fol-de-rol; he's too dignified." And with that there fell a sudden hush over the crowd, for which I was at a loss to account, till, upon looking up, I saw approaching on horseback, a young man in whom I had no difficulty in recognizing the subject of the last remark.

Straight, slight, elegant in appearance, but with an undoubted reserve of manner apparent even at a distance, he rode up to where I stood, and casting a slight glance around, bowed almost imperceptibly, and alighted. A boy caught the bridle of his horse, and Mr. Benson, without a word or further look, passed quickly into the office, leaving a silence behind him that was not disturbed till he returned with what was evidently his noonday mail. Remounting his horse, he stopped a moment to speak to a man who had just come up, and I seized the opportunity to study his face. I did not like it. It was handsome without doubt; the features were regular, the complexion fair, the expression gentlemanly if not commanding; but I did not like it. It was too impenetrable perhaps; and to a detective anxious to probe a man for his motives, this is ever a most fatal defect. His smile was without sunshine; his glance was an inquiry, a rebuke, a sarcasm, every thing but a revelation. As he rode away he carried with him the thought of all, yet I doubt if the admiration he undoubtedly inspired, was in a single case mixed with any warmer feeling than that of pride in a fellow townsman they could not understand. "Ice," thought I; "ice in all but its transparency!" So much for Benson the son.

The ball was to take place that very night; and the knowledge of this fact threw a different light over the letter I had read. The word mask had no longer any special significance, neither the word counterfeit, and yet such was the tenor of the note itself, and such the exaggerated nature of its phrases, I could not but feel that some plot of a reprehensible if not criminal nature was in the process of formation, which, as a rising young detective engaged in a mysterious and elusive search, it behooved me to know. And moved by this consideration, I turned to a new leaf in my memorandum-book, and put down in black and white the following facts thus summarily collected:

"A mysterious family with a secret.

"Rich, but with no visible means of wealth.

"Secluded, with no apparent reason for the same.

"A father who is a hermit.

"A son who is impenetrable.

"A daughter whose tastes are seldom gratified.

"The strange fact of a ball being given by this family after years of reserve and non-intercourse with their neighbors.

"The still stranger fact of it being a masquerade, a style of entertainment which, from its novelty and the opportunities it affords, makes this departure from ordinary rules seem marked and startling.

"The discovery of a letter appointing a rendezvous between two persons of the male sex, in the grounds of the party giving this ball, in which the opportunities afforded by a masquerade are to be used for forwarding some long-cherished scheme."

At the bottom of this I wrote a deduction:

"Some connection between one or more members of this family giving the ball, and the person called to the rendezvous; the entertainment being used as a blind if not as a means."

It was now four o'clock, five hours before the time of rendezvous. How should I employ the interval? A glance at the livery-stable hard by, determined me. Procuring a horse, I rode out on the road toward Mr. Benson's, for the purpose of reconnoitring the grounds; but as I proceeded I was seized by an intense desire to penetrate into the midst of this peculiar household, and judge for myself whether it was worth while to cherish any further suspicions in regard to this family. But how to effect such an entrance? What excuse could I give for my intrusion that would be likely to serve me on a day of such tumult and preoccupation? I looked up and down the road as if for inspiration. It did not come. Meanwhile, the huge trees that surrounded the house had loomed in sight, and presently the beauties of lawn and parterre began to appear beyond the high iron fence, through which I could catch now and then short glimpses of hurrying forms, as lanterns were hung on the trees and all things put in readiness for the evening's entertainment. Suddenly a thought struck me. If Mr. Benson was the man they said, he was not engaged in any of these arrangements. Mr. Benson was a hermit. Now what could I say that would interest a hermit? I racked my brains; a single idea came. It was daring in its nature, but what of that! The gate must be passed, Mr. Benson must be seen—or so my adventurous curiosity decided,—and to do it, something must be ventured. Taking out my card, which was simply inscribed with my name, I wrote on it, "Business private and immediate," and assuming my most gentlemanly and inoffensive manner, rode calmly through the gate to the front of the house. If I had been on foot I doubt if I would have been allowed to pass by the servant lounging about in that region, but the horse carried me through in more senses than one, and almost before I realized it, I found myself pausing before the portico, in full view of a dozen or more busy men and boys.

Imitating the manner of Mr. Benson at the post-office, I jumped from my horse and threw the bridle to the boy nearest me. Instantly and before I could take a step, a servant issued from the open door, and with an expression of anxiety somewhat surprising under the circumstances, took his stand before me in a way to hinder my advance.

"Mr. Benson does not receive visitors to-day," said he.

"I am not a visitor," replied I; "I have business with Mr. Benson," and I handed him my card, which he looked at with a doubtful expression.

"Mr. Benson's commands are not to be disobeyed," persisted the man. "My master sees no one to-day."

"But this is an exceptional case," I urged, my curiosity rising at this unexpected opposition. "My business is important and concerns him. He cannot refuse to see me."

The servant shook his head with what appeared to me to be an unnecessary expression of alarm, but nevertheless retreated a step, allowing me to enter. "I will call Mr. Hartley," cried he.

But that was just what I did not wish. It was Benson the father I had come to see, and I was not to be baffled in this way.

"Mr. Hartley won't do," said I, in my lowest but most determined accents. "If Mr. Benson is not ill, I must beg to be admitted to his presence." And stepping inside the small reception room at my right, I sat down on the first chair I came to.

The man stood for a moment confounded at my pertinacity, then with a last scrutinizing look, that took in every detail of my person and apparel, drew slowly off, shaking his head and murmuring to himself.

Meanwhile the mingled splendor and elegance of my surroundings were slowly making their impression upon me. The hall by which I had entered was spacious and imposing; the room in which I sat, a model of beauty in design and finish. I was allowing myself the luxury of studying its pictures and numerous works of art, when the sound of voices reached my ear from the next room. A man and woman were conversing there in smothered tones, but my senses are very acute, and I had no difficulty in overhearing what was said.

"Oh, what an exciting day this has been!" cried the female voice. "I have wanted to ask you a dozen times what you think of it all. Will he succeed this time? Has he the nerve to embrace his opportunity, or what is more, the tact to make one? Failure now would be fatal. Father—"

"Hush!" broke in the other voice, in a masculine tone of repressed intensity. "Do not forget that success depends upon your prudence. One whisper of what you are about, and the whole scheme is destroyed."

"I will be careful; only do you think that all is going well and as we planned it?"

"It will not be my fault if it does not," was the reply, uttered with an accent so sinister I was conscious of a violent surprise when, in the next instant, the other, with a burst of affectionate fervor, cried in an ardent tone:

"Oh, how good you are, and what a comfort you are to me!"

I was just pondering over the incongruity thus presented, when the servant returned with my card.

"Mr. Benson wishes to know the nature of your business," said he, in a voice I was uncomfortably conscious must penetrate to the next room and awake its inmates to a knowledge of my proximity.

"Let me have the card," said I; and taking it, I added to my words the simple phrase, "On behalf of the Constable of the town," remembering I had heard the postmaster say this position was held by his brother. "There," said I, "carry that back to your master."

The servant took the card, glanced down at the words I had written, started and hastily drew back. "You had better come," said he, leading the way into the hall.

I was only too glad to comply; in fact, escape from that room seemed imperative. But just as I was crossing the threshold, a sudden, quick cry, half joyful, half fearful, rose behind me, and turning, I met the eyes of a young lady peering upon me from a lifted portière, with an expression of mingled terror and longing that would have astonished me greatly, if it had not instantly disappeared at the first sight of my face.

"Pardon me," she exclaimed, drawing back with an embarrassed movement into the room from which she had emerged. But soon recovering herself, she stepped hastily forward, and ignoring me, said to the servant at my side: "Jonas, who is this gentleman, and where are you taking him?"

With a bow, Jonas replied: "He comes on business, miss, and Mr. Benson consents to see him."

"But I thought my father had expressly commanded that no one was to be allowed to enter the library to-day," she exclaimed, but in a musing tone that asked for no response. And hastily as we passed down the hall, I could not escape the uneasy sense that her eager eyes were following us as we went.

"Too much emotion for so small a matter, and a strange desire on the part of every one to keep Mr. Benson from being intruded upon to-day," was my mental comment. And I was scarcely surprised when upon our arrival at the library door we found it locked. However, a knock, followed by a few whispered words on the part of the servant, served to arouse the hermit within, and with a quick turn of the key, the door flew back on its hinges, and the master of the house stood before me.

It was a moment to be remembered: first, because the picture presented to my eyes was of a marked and impressive character; and secondly, because something in the expression of the gentleman before me showed that he had received a shock at my introduction which was not to be expected after the pains which had been taken to prepare his mind for my visit. He was a tall, remarkable-looking man, with a head already whitened, and a form which, if not bowed, had only retained its upright carriage by means of the indomitable will that betrayed itself in his eyes. Seen against the rich background of the stained-glass window that adorned one end of the apartment, his stern, furrowed face and eagerly repellant aspect imprinted itself upon me like a silhouette, while the strong emotion I could not but detect in his bearing, lent to the whole a poetic finish that made it a living picture which, as I have said, I have never been able to forget.

"You have come from the constable of the town," said he, in a firm, hard tone, impressive as his look. "May I ask for what purpose?"

Looking around, I saw the servant had disappeared. "Sir," said I, gathering up my courage, as I became convinced that in this case I had a thoroughly honest man to deal with, "you are going to give a fancy ball to-night. Such an event is a novelty in these parts, and arouses much curiosity. Some of the men about town have even been heard to threaten to leap the fences and steal a look at your company, whether you will or not. Mr. White wants to know whether you need any assistance in keeping the grounds clear of all but your legitimate guests; if so, he is ready to supply whatever force you may need."

"Mr. White is very kind," returned Mr. Benson, in a voice which, despite his will-power, showed that his agitation had in some unaccountable way been increased by my communication. "I had not thought of any such contingency," he murmured, moving over to a window and looking out. "An invasion of rowdies would not be agreeable. They might even find their way into the house." He paused and cast a sudden look at me. "Who are you?" he abruptly asked.

The question took me by surprise, but I answered bravely if not calmly: "I am a man who sometimes assists Mr. White in the performance of his duties, and in case you need it, will be the one to render you assistance to-night. A line to Mr. White, if you doubt me—"

A wave of his meagre hand stopped me. "Do you think you could keep out of my house to-night, any one I did not wish to enter?" he asked.

"I should at least like to try."

"A ticket is given to every invited guest; but if men are going to climb the fences, tickets will amount to but little."

"I will see that the fences are guarded," cried I, gratified at the prospect of being allowed upon the scene of action. "I can hinder any one from coming in that way, if—" Here I paused, conscious of something, I could hardly say what, that bade me be cautious and weigh my words well. "If you desire it and will give me the authority to act for you," I added in a somewhat more indifferent tone.

"I do desire it," he replied shortly, moving over to the table and taking up a card. "Here is a ticket that will insure you entrance into the grounds; the rest you will manage without scandal. I do not want any disturbance, but if you see any one hanging about the house or peering into the windows or attempting to enter in any way except through the front door, you are to arrest them, no matter who they are. I have an especial reason for desiring my wishes attended to in this regard," he went on, not noticing the preoccupation that had seized me, "and will pay well if on the morrow I find that every thing has gone off according to my desires."

"Money is a powerful incentive to duty," I rejoined, with marked emphasis, directing a sly glance at the mirror opposite, in whose depths I had but a moment before been startled by the sudden apparition of the pale and strongly agitated face of young Mr. Benson, who was peering from a door-way half hidden by a screen at our back. "I will be on hand to-night." And with what I meant to be a cynical look, I made my bow and disappeared from the room.

As I expected, I was met at the front door by Mr. Hartley. "A word with you," said he. "Jonas tells me you are from the constable of the town. May I ask what has gone amiss that you come here to disturb my father on a day like this?"

His tone was not unkind, his expression not without suavity. If I had not had imprinted on my memory the startling picture of his face as I had seen it an instant before in the mirror, I should have been tempted to believe in his goodness and integrity at this moment. As it was, I doubted him through and through, yet replied with frankness and showed him the ticket I had received from his father.

"And you are going to make it your business to guard the grounds to-night?" he asked, gloomily glancing at the card in my hand as if he would like to annihilate it.

"Yes," said I.

He drew me into a small room half filled with plants.

"Now," said he, "see here. Such a piece of interference is entirely uncalled for, and you have been alarming my father unnecessarily. There are no rowdies in this town, and if one or two of the villagers should get into the grounds, where is the harm? They cannot get into the house even if they wanted to, which they don't. I do not wish this, our first show of hospitality, to assume a hostile aspect, and whatever my father's expectations may be, I must request you to curtail your duties as much as possible and limit them to responding by your presence when called upon."

"But your father has a right to expect the fullest obedience to his wishes," I protested. "He would not be satisfied if I should do no more than you request, and I cannot afford to disappoint him."

He looked at me with a calculating eye, and I expected to see him put his hand in his pocket; but Hartley Benson played his cards better than that. "Very well," said he, "if you persist in regarding my father's wishes as paramount, I have nothing to say. Fulfil your duties as you conceive them, but don't look for my support if any foolish misadventure makes you ashamed of yourself." And drawing back, he motioned me out of the room.

I felt I had received a check, and hurried out of the house. But scarcely had I entered upon the walk that led down to the gate, when I heard a light step behind me. Turning, I encountered the pretty daughter of the house, the youthful Miss Carrie.

"Wait," she cried, allowing herself to display her emotion freely in face and bearing. "I have heard who you are from my brother," she continued, approaching me with a soft grace that at once put me upon my guard. "Now, tell me who are the rowdies that threaten to invade our grounds?"

"I do not know their names, miss," I responded; "but they are a rough-looking set you would not like to see among your guests."

"There are no very rough-looking men in our village," she declared; "you must be mistaken in regard to them. My father is nervous and easily alarmed. It was wrong to arouse his fears."

I thought of that steady eye of his, of force sufficient to hold in awe a regiment of insurgents, and smiled at her opinion of my understanding.

"Then you do not wish the grounds guarded," I said, in as indifferent a tone as I could assume.

"I do not consider it necessary."

"But I have already pledged myself to fulfil your father's commands."

"I know," she said, drawing a step nearer, with a most enchanting smile. "And that was right under the circumstances; but we, his children, who may be presumed to know more of social matters than a recluse,—I, especially," she added, with a certain emphasis, "tell you it is not necessary. We fear the scandal it may cause; besides, some of the guests may choose to linger about the grounds under the trees, and would be rather startled at being arrested as intruders."

"What, then, do you wish me to do?" I asked, leaning toward her, with an appearance of yielding.

"To accept this money," she murmured, blushing, "and confine yourself to-night to remaining in the background unless called upon."

This was a seconding of her brother's proposition with a vengeance. Taking the purse she handed me, I weighed it for a moment in my hand, and then slowly shook my head. "Impossible," I cried; "but"—and I fixed my eyes intently upon her countenance—"if there is any one in particular whom you desire me to ignore, I am ready to listen to a description of his person. It has always been my pleasure to accommodate myself as much as possible to the whims of the ladies."

It was a bold stroke that might have cost me the game. Indeed, I half expected she would raise her voice and order some of the men about her to eject me from the grounds. But instead of that she remained for a moment blushing painfully, but surveying me with an unfaltering gaze that reminded me of her father's.

"There is a person," said she, in a low, restrained voice, "whom I am especially anxious should remain unmolested, whatever he may or may not be seen to do. He is a guest," she went on, a sudden pallor taking the place of her blushes, "and has a right to be here; but I doubt if he at once enters the house, and I even suspect he may choose to loiter awhile in the grounds before attempting to join the company. I ask you to allow him to do so."

I bowed with an appearance of great respect. "Describe him," said I.

For a moment she faltered, with a distressed look I found it difficult to understand. Then, with a sudden glance over my person, exclaimed: "Look in the glass when you get home and you will see the fac-simile of his form, though not of his face. He is fair, whereas you are dark." And with a haughty lift of her head calculated to rob me of any satisfaction I might have taken in her words, she stepped slowly back.

I stopped her with a gesture. "Miss," said I, "take your purse before you go. Payment of any service I may render your father will come in time. This affair is between you and me, and I hope I am too much of a gentleman to accept money for accommodating a lady in so small a matter as this."

But she shook her head. "Take it," said she, "and assure me that I may rely on you."

"You may rely on me without the money," I replied, forcing the purse back into her hand.

"Then I shall rest easy," she returned, and retreated with a lightsome air toward the house.

The next moment I was on the highway with my thoughts. What did it all mean? Was it, then, a mere love affair across which I had foolishly stumbled, and was I busying myself unnecessarily about a rendezvous that might mean no more than an elopement from under a severe father's eye? Taking out the note which had led to all these efforts on my part, I read it for the third time.

"All goes well. The time has come; every thing is in train, and success is certain. Be in the shrubbery at the northeast corner of the grounds at 9 P.M. precisely; you will be given a mask and such other means as are necessary to insure you the accomplishment of the end you have in view. He cannot hold out against a surprise. The word by which you will know your friends is COUNTERFEIT."

A love-letter of course; and I had been a fool to suppose it any thing else. The young people are to surprise the old gentleman in the presence of their friends. They have been secretly married perhaps, who knows, and take this method of obtaining a public reconciliation. But that word "Counterfeit," and the sinister tone of Hartley Benson as he said: "It shall not fail through lack of effort on my part!" Such a word and such a tone did not rightly tally with this theory. Few brothers take such interest in their sister's love affairs as to grow saturnine over them. There was, beneath all this, something which I had not yet penetrated. Meantime my duty led me to remain true to the one person of whose integrity of purpose I was most thoroughly convinced.

Returning to the village, I hunted up Mr. White and acquainted him with what I had undertaken in his name; and then perceiving that the time was fast speeding by, strolled over to the tavern for my supper.

The stranger was still there, walking up and down the sitting-room. He joined us at the table, but I observed he scarcely tasted his food, and both then and afterward manifested the same anxious suspense that had characterized his movements from the time of our first encounter.

CHAPTER II

THE BLACK DOMINO

At half past eight I was at my post. The mysterious stranger, still under my direct surveillance, had already entered the grounds and taken his stand in the southwest corner of the shrubbery, thereby leaving me free to exercise my zeal in keeping the fences and gates free of intruders. At nine the guests were nearly if not all assembled; and promptly at the hour mentioned in the note so often referred to, I stole away from my post and hid myself amid the bushes that obscured the real place of rendezvous.

It was a retired spot, eminently fitted for a secret meeting. The lamps, which had been hung in profusion through the grounds, had been studiously excluded from this quarter. Even the broad blaze of light that poured from the open doors and windows of the brilliantly illuminated mansion, sent no glimmer through the broad belt of evergreens that separated this retreat from the open lawn beyond. All was dark, all was mysterious, all was favorable to the daring plan I had undertaken. In silence I awaited the sound of approaching steps.

My suspense was of short duration. In a few moments I heard a low rustle in the bushes near me, then a form appeared before my eyes, and a man's voice whispered:

"Is there any one here?"

My reply was to glide quietly into view.

Instantly he spoke again, this time with more assurance.

"Are you ready for a counterfeit?"

"I am ready for any thing," I returned, in smothered tones, hoping by thus disguising my voice, to lure him into a revelation of the true purpose of this mysterious rendezvous.

But instead of the explanations I expected, the person before me made a quick movement, and I felt a domino thrown over my shoulders.

"Draw it about you well," he murmured; "there are lynx eyes in the crowd to-night." And while I mechanically obeyed, he bent down to my ear and earnestly continued: "Now listen, and be guided by my instructions. You will not be able to enter by the front door, as it is guarded, and you cannot pass without removing your mask. But the window on the left-hand balcony is at your service. It is open, and the man appointed to keep intruders away, has been bribed to let you pass. Once inside the house, join the company sans céremonie; and do not hesitate to converse with any one who addresses you by the countersign. Promptly at ten o'clock look around you for a domino in plain black. When you see him move, follow him, but with discretion, so that you may not seem to others to be following. Sooner or later he will pause and point to a closed door. Notice that door, and when your guide has disappeared, approach and enter it without fear or hesitation. You will find yourself in a small apartment connecting with the library.

"There is but one thing more to say. If the wineglass you will observe on the library table smells of wine, you may know your father has had his nightly potion and gone to bed. But if it contains nothing more than a small white powder, you may be certain he has yet to return to the library, and that by waiting, you will have the long-wished-for opportunity of seeing him."

And pausing for no reply, my strange companion suddenly thrust a mask into my hand and darted from the circle of trees that surrounded us.

For a moment I stood dumbfounded at the position in which my recklessness had placed me. All the folly, the impertinence even, of the proceeding upon which I had entered, was revealed to me in its true colors, and I mentally inquired what could have induced me to thus hamper myself with the details of a mystery so entirely removed from the serious matter I had in charge. Resolved to abandon the affair, I made a hasty attempt to disengage myself from the domino in which I had been so unceremoniously enveloped. But invisible hands seemed to restrain me. A vivid remembrance of the tone in which these final instructions had been uttered returned to my mind, and while I recognized the voice as that of Hartley Benson, I also recognized the almost saturnine intensity of expression which had once before imbued his words with a significance both forcible and surprising. The secret, if a purely family one, was of no ordinary nature; and at the thought I felt my old interest revive. All the excuses with which I had hitherto silenced my conscience recurred to me with fresh force, and mechanically donning my mask, I prepared to follow out my guide's instructions to the last detail.

The window to which I had been directed stood wide open. Through it came the murmur of music and the hum of gay voices. Visions of a motley crowd decked in grotesque costumes passed constantly before my eyes. Sight and sound combined to allure me. Hurrying to the window, I stepped carelessly in.

A low guttural "Hugh!" at once greeted me. It was from a mask in full Indian costume, whom I saw leaning with a warrior's well-known dignity against the embrasure of the window by which I had entered. Giving him a scrutinizing glance, I came to the conclusion he was a young and not inelegant man; and impelled by a reasonable curiosity as to how I looked myself, I cast my eyes down upon my own person. I found my appearance sufficiently striking. The domino, in which I was wrapped was of a brilliant yellow hue, covered here and there with black figures representing all sorts of fantastic creatures, from hobgoblins of a terrible type, to merry Kate Greenaway silhouettes. "Humph!" thought I, "it seems I am not destined to glide unnoticed amid the crowd."

The first person who approached me was a gay little shepherdess.

"Ah, ha!" was the sportive exclamation with which she greeted me. "Here is one of my wandering sheep!" And with a laugh, she endeavored to hook me to her side by means of her silver crook.

But this blithesome puppet possessed no interest for me. So with a growl and a bound I assured her I was nothing more than a wolf in sheep's clothing, and would eat her up if she did not run away; at which she gayly laughed and vanished, and for a moment I was left alone. But only for a moment. A masked lady, whom I had previously observed standing upright and solitary in a distant corner of the room, now approached, and taking me by the arm, led me eagerly to one side.

"Oh, Joe!" she whispered, "is it you? How glad I am to have you here, and how I hope we are going to be happy at last!"

Fearing to address a person seemingly so well acquainted with the young man whose place I had usurped, I merely pressed, with most perfidious duplicity, the little hand that was so confidingly clasped in mine. It seemed to satisfy her, for she launched at once into ardent speech.

"Oh, Joe, I have been so anxious to have you with us once again! Hartley is a good brother, but he is not my old playmate. Then father will be so much happier if you only succeed in making him forget the past."

Seeing by this that it was Miss Carrie Benson with whom I had to deal, I pressed the little hand again, and tenderly drew her closer to my side. That I felt all the time like a villain of the blackest dye, it is quite unnecessary for me to state.

"Has Hartley told you just what you are to do?" was her next remark. "Father is very determined not to relent and has kept himself locked in his library all day, for fear you should force yourself upon his presence. I could never have gained his consent to give this ball if I had not first persuaded him it would serve as a means to keep you at a distance; that if you saw the house thronged with guests, natural modesty would restrain you from pushing yourself forward. I think he begins to distrust his own firmness. He fears he will melt at the sight of you. He has been failing this last year and—" A sudden choke stopped her voice.

I was at once both touched and alarmed; touched at the grief which showed her motives to be pure and good, and alarmed at the position in which I had thrust myself to the apparent detriment of these same laudable motives. Moved by a desire to right matters, I ventured to speak:

"And do you think," I whispered, in purposely smothered accents, "that if he sees me he will relent?"

"I am sure of it. He yearns over you, Joe; and if he had not sworn never to speak to you again, he would have sent for you long ago. Hartley believes as well as I that the time for reconciliation has come."

"And is Hartley," I ventured again, not without a secret fear of the consequences, "really anxious for reconciliation?"

"Oh, Joe! can you doubt it? Has he not striven from the first to make father forget? Would he encourage you to come here to-night, furnish you with a disguise, and consent to act both as your champion and adviser, if he did not want to see you and father friends again? You don't understand Hartley; you never have. You would not have repelled his advances so long, if you had realized how truly he had forgiven every thing and forgotten it. Hartley has the pride of a person who has never done wrong himself. But even pride gives way before brotherly affection; and you have suffered so much and so long, poor Joe!"

"So, so," thought I, "Joe is then the aggressor!" And for a moment, I longed to be the man I represented, if only to clasp this dear little sister in my arms and thank her for her goodness. "You are a darling," I faintly articulated, inwardly determined to rush forthwith into the garden, hand over my domino to the person for whom it was intended, and make my escape from a scene which I had so little right to enjoy. But at this instant an interruption occurred which robbed me of my companion, but kept me effectually in my place. A black domino swept by us, dragging Miss Benson from my side, while at the same time a harsh voice whispered in my ear:

"To counterfeit wrong when one is right, necessarily opens one to misunderstanding."

I started, recognizing in this mode of speech a friend, and therefore one from whom I could not escape without running the risk of awakening suspicion.

"That is true," I returned, hoping by my abrupt replies to cut short this fresh colloquy and win a speedy release.

But something in my answer roused the interest of the person at my side, and caused a display of emotion that led to quite an opposite result from what I desired.

"You awaken a thousand conjectures in my mind by that reply," exclaimed my friend, edging me a little farther back from the crowd. "I have always had my doubts about—about—" he paused, hunting for the proper phrase—"about your having done what they said," he somewhat lamely concluded. "It was so unlike you. But now I begin to see the presence of a possibility that might perhaps explain much we never understood. Joe, my boy, you never said you were innocent, but—"

"Who are you?" I asked boldly, peering into the twinkling eyes that shone upon me from his sedate mask. "In the discussion of such matters as these, it would be dreadful to make a mistake."

"And don't you recognize your Uncle Joe?" he asked, with a certain plaintive reproach somewhat out of keeping with his costume of "potent, grave, and reverend signior." "I came over from Hollowell on purpose, because Carrie intimated that you were going to make one final effort to see your father. Edith is here too," he murmured, thrusting his face alarmingly near mine. "She would not stay away, though we were all afraid she might betray herself; her emotions are so quick. Poor child! she never doubted you; and if my suspicions are correct—"

"Edith?" I interrupted,—"Edith?" An Edith was the last person I desired to meet under these circumstances. "Where is she?" I tremulously inquired, starting aside in some dismay at the prospect of encountering this unknown quantity of love and devotion.

But my companion, seizing me by the arm, drew me back. "She is not far away; of that you may be sure. But it will never do for you to try and hunt her up. You would not know her in her mask. Besides, if you remain still she will come to you."

That was just what I feared, but upon looking round and seeing no suspicious-looking damsel anywhere near me, I concluded to waive my apprehensions on her account and proceed to the development of an idea that had been awakened by the old gentleman's words.

"You are right," I acquiesced, edging, in my turn, toward the curtained recess of a window near by. "Let us wait here, and meantime you shall tell me what your suspicions are, for I feel the time has come for the truth to be made known, and who could better aid me in proclaiming it than you who have always stood my friend?"

"That is true," he murmured, all eagerness at once. Then in a lower tone and with a significant gesture: "There is something, then, which has never been made known? Edith was right when she said you did not steal the bonds out of your father's desk?"

As he paused and looked me in the face, I was obliged to make some reply. I chose one of the non-committal sort.

"Don't ask me!" I murmured, turning away with every appearance of profound agitation.

He did not suspect the ruse.

"But, my boy, I shall have to ask you; if I am to help you out of this scrape, I must know the truth. Yet if it is as I suspect, I can see why you should hesitate even now. You are a generous fellow, Joe, but even generosity can be carried past its proper limits."

"Uncle," I exclaimed, leaning over him and whispering tremulously in his ear, "what are your suspicions? If I hear you give utterance to them, perhaps it will not be so hard for me to speak."

He hesitated, looked all about us with a questioning glance, put his mouth to my ear, and whispered:

"If I should use the name of Hartley in connection with what I have to say, would you be so very much surprised?"

With a quick semblance of emotion, I drew back.

"You think—" I tremulously commenced, and as suddenly broke off.

"That it was he who did it, and that you, knowing how your father loved him and built his hopes upon him, bore the blame of it yourself."

"Ha!" I exclaimed, with a deep breath as of relief. The suspicions of Uncle Joe were worth hearing.

He seemed to be satisfied with the ejaculation, and with an increase of eagerness in his tone, went quickly on:

"Am I not right, my boy? Is not this the secret of your whole conduct from that dreadful day to this?"

"Don't ask me," I again pleaded, taking care, however, to draw a step nearer and exclaim in almost the same breath: "Why should you think it must necessarily have been one of us? What did you know that you should be so positive it was either he or I who committed this dishonest action?"

"What did I know? Why, what everybody else did. That your father, hearing a noise in his study one night, rose up quietly and slipped to the door of communication in time to hear a stealthy foot leave the room and proceed down the hall toward the apartment usually occupied by you and your brother; that, alarmed and filled with vague distrust, he at once lit the lamp, only to discover his desk had been forcibly broken into and a number of coupon bonds taken out; that, struck to the heart, he went immediately to the room where you and your brother lay, found him lying quiet, and to all appearance asleep, while you looked flushed and with difficulty met his eye; that without hesitation he thereupon accused you of theft, and began to search the apartment; that he found the bonds, as we both know, in a cupboard at the head of your bed, and when you were asked if you had put them there you remained silent, and neither then nor afterward made any denial of being the one who stole them."

A mournful "Yes" was all the reply I ventured upon.

"Now it never seemed to occur to your father to doubt your guilt. The open window and the burglar's jimmy found lying on the floor of the study, being only so many proofs, to his mind, of your deep calculation and great duplicity. But I could not help thinking, even on that horrible morning, that your face did not wear a look of guilt so much as it did that of firm and quiet resolution. But I was far from suspecting the truth, my boy, or I should never have allowed you to fall a victim to your father's curse, and be sent forth like a criminal from home and kindred. If only for Edith's sake I would have spoken— dear, trusting, faithful girl that she is!"

"But—but—" I brokenly ejaculated, anxious to gain as much of the truth as was possible in the few minutes allotted me; "what has awakened your suspicions at this late day? Why should you doubt Hartley now, if you did not then?"

"Well, I cannot really say. Perhaps Edith's persistent aversion to your brother has had something to do with it. Then he has grown cold and hard, while you have preserved your boyish freshness and affection. I—I don't like him, that is the truth; and with my dislike arose doubts, and—and—well, I cannot tell how it is, but I will believe you if you say he was the one to blame in this matter; and what is more, your father will believe you too; for he does not feel the same satisfaction in Hartley's irreproachable character that he used to, and—and—"

A sudden movement in the crowd stopped him. A tall, graceful-looking woman clad entirely in white had just entered the room and seemed to be making her way toward us.

"There is Edith!" he declared. "She is hunting for the yellow domino ornamented with black that she has been told conceals her lover. Shall I go and fetch her here, or will you wait until she spies you of her own accord?"

"I will wait," I uneasily replied, edging nearer to the window with the determination of using it as a means of escape if my companion only gave me the chance. "See! she is in the hands of an old Jew, who seems to be greatly taken with the silver trimmings on her sleeves. Suppose you improve the opportunity to slip away," I laughingly suggested. "Lovers' meetings are not usually of an order to interest third parties."

"Aren't they, you rogue!" retorted the old gentleman, giving me a jocose poke in the ribs. "Well, well, I suppose you are right. But you have not told me—"

"I will tell you every thing in an hour," I hastily assured him. "I am going to meet my father in the library, and after he has heard the truth, you shall be admitted and all will be explained."

"That is only fair," he replied. "Your father has the first rights, of course. But Joe, my boy, remember I am not over and above patient of disposition, and don't keep me waiting too long." And with an affectionate squeeze of my hand, he stepped out from the recess where we stood and made his way once more into the throng.

No sooner had he left my side than I threw up the window. "Now is the time for the real Joe to appear upon the scene," was my mental decision. "I have done for him what he as a gentleman would probably never do for himself—pumped this old party and got every thing in trim for Hartley's discomfiture. But the courting business is another matter; also the interview with the outraged father in the library. That cannot be done by proxy; so here goes for a change of actors."

And with reckless disregard of consequences, I prepared to jump from the window, when a sudden light flashed over the lawn beneath and I saw I was at least twelve feet from the ground.

"Well," I exclaimed, drawing hastily back; "such a leap as that is too much to expect of any man!" And with the humiliating consciousness of being caught in a trap, I proceeded to close the window.

"Joe!"

'Twas a low whisper, but how thrilling! Turning, I greeted, with the show of fervor I considered necessary to the occasion, the white-veiled lady who had glided into my retreat.

"Did you think I was never coming, Joe? Everybody who could get in my way certainly managed to do so. Then Hartley is so suspicious, and followed me with his eyes so persistently, I did not dare show my designs too plainly. It is only this minute he left my side. If you had been anywhere else I do not know as I should have succeeded even now in getting a word with you—oh!"

This exclamation was called forth by a sudden movement that took place near us. The curtain was drawn back and a tall man dressed in a black domino glanced in, gave us a scrutinizing look, bowed, and dropped the curtain again.

"Hartley," she whisperingly explained.

I took her by the hand; there was no help for it; gesture and a lover-like demeanor must, in this case, supply the place of speech.

"Hush!" she entreated. (Not that I had spoken.) "I dare not stay. When you have seen your father, perhaps I will have courage to join you; but now it would be better for me to go." And her eyes roamed toward the curtain, while the little hand I held in mine grew cold and slightly trembled.

I pressed that little hand, but, as you may well believe, did not urge her to remain. Yet she did not seem in a hurry to depart, and I do not know what complications might have ensued, if another movement in the curtain had not reawakened her fears and caused her, notwithstanding her evident reluctance, to start quickly away.

I did not linger long behind her. Scarcely had the curtain fallen from her hand than I stepped hastily forth. But alas for my hopes of escape! No sooner had I joined the group of merry-makers circling about the open door, than I felt a touch on my arm, and looking up, saw before me the Black Domino. The hour of ten had struck and my guide to the library was at hand. There was no alternative left me but to follow him.

CHAPTER III

AN UNEXPECTED CALAMITY

Five minutes passed, during which I threaded more laughing groups and sauntered down more mysterious passage-ways than I would care to count. Still the mysterious Black Domino glided on before me, leading me from door to door till my patience was nearly exhausted, and I had well-nigh determined to give him the slip and make my way at once to the garden, and the no-doubt-by-this-time-highly-impatient Joe.

But before I had the opportunity of carrying out this scheme, the ominous Black Domino paused, and carelessly pointing to a door at the termination of a narrow corridor, bowed, and hastily withdrew.

"Now," said I, as soon as I found myself alone, "shall I proceed with this farce, or shall I end it? To go on means to interview Mr. Benson, acquaint him with what has come to my knowledge during the last half hour in which I have so successfully personified his son, and by these means perhaps awake him to the truth concerning this serious matter of Joseph's innocence or Hartley's guilt; while to stop now implies nothing more nor less than a full explanation with his son, a man of whose character, manners, and disposition I know little or nothing."

Either alternative presented infinite difficulties, but of the two the former seemed to me more feasible and less embarrassing. At all events, in talking with Mr. Benson, I should not have the sensibilities of a lover to contend with, and however unfortunate in its results our interview might be, would be at the mercy of old blood instead of young, a point always to be considered in a case where one's presumption has been carried beyond the bounds of decorum.

Unlocking the door, I stepped, as I had been told I should, into a small room adjoining the library. All around me were books. Even the door by which I had entered was laden with them, so that when it was closed, all vestige of the door itself disappeared. Across the opening into the library stood a screen, and it was not until I had pushed this somewhat aside that I was able to look into that room.

My first glance assured me it was empty. Stark and bare of any occupant, the high-backed chairs loomed in the funereal gloom, while on the table, toward which I inadvertently glanced, stood a decanter with a solitary wineglass at its side. Instantly I remembered what had been told me concerning that glass, and stepping forward, I took it up and looked at it.

Immediately I heard, or thought I heard, an exclamation uttered somewhere near me. But upon glancing up and down the room and perceiving no one, I concluded I was mistaken, and deliberately proceeded to examine the wineglass and assure myself that no wine had as yet been poured upon the powder I found in it. Satisfied at last that Mr. Benson had not yet taken his usual evening potion, I put the glass back and withdrew again to my retreat.

I do not think another minute could have elapsed, before I heard a step in the room behind me. A door leading into an adjoining apartment had opened and Mr. Benson had come in. He passed immediately to the table, poured out the wine upon the powder, and drank it off without a moment's hesitation. I heard him sigh as he put the glass down.

With a turn of my hand I slipped off both domino and mask, and prepared to announce my presence by tapping on the lintel of the door beside which I stood. But a sudden change in Mr. Benson's lofty figure startled me. He was swaying, and the arms which had fallen to his side were moving with a convulsive action that greatly alarmed me. But almost instantly he recovered himself, and paced with a steady step toward the hall door, which at that moment resounded with a short loud knock.

"Who is there?" he asked, with every appearance of his usual sternness.

"Hartley," was the reply.

"Are you alone?" the old gentleman again queried, making a move as if to unlock the door.

"Carrie is with me; no one else," came in smothered accents from without.

Mr. Benson at once turned the key, but no sooner had he done so than he staggered back. For an instant or two of horror he stood oscillating from side to side, then his frame succumbed, and the terrified eyes of his children beheld his white head lying low, all movement and appearance of life gone from the form that but a moment before towered so proudly before them.

With a shriek, the daughter flung herself down at his side, and even the cheek of Hartley Benson grew white as he leaned over his father's already inanimate body.

"He is dead!" came in a wild cry from her lips. "See! he does not breathe. Oh! Hartley, what could have happened? Do you think that Joe—"

"Hush!" he exclaimed, with a furtive glance around him. "He may be here; let me look. If Joe has done this—" He did not continue, but rose, and with a rapid tread began to cross the floor in my direction.

In a flash I realized my situation. To be found by him now, without a domino, and in the position of listener, would be any thing but desirable. But I knew of no way of escape, or so for the moment it seemed. But great emergencies call forth sudden resources. In the quick look I inadvertently threw around me, I observed that the portière hanging between me and the library was gathered at one side in very heavy folds. If I could hide behind them perhaps I might elude the casual glance he would probably cast into my place of concealment. At all events it was worth trying, and at the thought I glided behind the curtain. I was not disappointed in my calculations. Arrived at the door, he looked in, perceived the domino lying in a heap on the floor, and immediately drew back with an exclamation of undoubted satisfaction.

"He is gone," said he, crossing back to his sister's side. Then in a tone of mingled irony and bitterness, hard to describe, cried aloud with a glance toward the open door: "He has first killed his father and then fled. Fool that I was to think he could be trusted!"

A horrified "Hartley!" burst from his sister's lips and a suppressed but equally vehement "Villain!" from mine; but neither of us had time for more, for almost at the same instant the room filled with frightened guests, among which I discerned the face and form of the old servant Jonas, and the flowing robes and the white garments of Uncle Joe and the graceful Edith.

To describe the confusion that followed would be beyond my powers, especially as my attention was at the time not so much directed to the effect produced by this catastrophe, as to the man whom, from the moment Mr. Benson fell to the floor, I regarded as my lawful prey. He did not quake and lose his presence of mind in this terrible crisis. He was gifted with too much self-control to betray any unseemly agitation even over such a matter as his father's sudden death. Once only did I detect his lip tremble, and that was when an elderly gentleman (presumably a doctor) exclaimed after a careful examination of the fallen man:

"This is no case of apoplexy, gentlemen!"

Then indeed Mr. Hartley Benson shivered, and betrayed an emotion for which I considered myself as receiving a due explanation when, a few minutes later, I observed the same gentleman lay his hand upon the decanter and glass that stood on the table, and after raising them one after the other to his nose, slowly shake his head, and with a furtive look around him, lock them both in a small cupboard that opened over the mantel-piece.

CHAPTER IV

IN THE LIBRARY

Mr. Benson was really dead. The fact being announced, most of the guests withdrew. In ten minutes after he fell, the room was comparatively clear. Only the various members of the family, together with the gentleman I have already mentioned, remained behind; and, even of these, the two ladies were absent, they having followed the body into the adjoining room, where it had been reverently carried by the attached Jonas and another servant whose face I did not see.

"A most unlooked-for catastrophe," burst from the lips of Uncle Joe. "Did you ever suspect he was a victim to heart disease?" he now asked, this time with looks directed toward the doctor.

"No," came from that gentleman in a short, sharp way, which made Hartley Benson's pale face flush, though his eye did not waver from its steady solemn look toward the door through which his father's form had just been carried. "Mr. Benson was sound through and through a month ago. I know, because I examined him previous to his making his will. There was no heart disease then; that I am ready to take my oath upon."

Hartley Benson's rigid look unfastened itself from the door and turned slowly toward the sombre face of the speaker, while Uncle Joe, with an increased expression of distress, looked slowly around as if he half hoped, half feared to behold his favorite nephew advance upon them from some shadowy corner.

"My father consulted you, then?" said the former, in his slow, reserved way. "Did not that evince some suspicion of disease on his part?"

"Possibly; a man in a despondent frame of mind will often imagine he has some deadly complaint or other. But he was quite sound; too sound, he seemed to think. Your father was not a happy man, Mr. Benson."

There was meaning in the tone, and I was not surprised to observe Hartley draw back. "Why," said he, "do you think—"

"I think nothing," broke in the doctor; "only"—and here he brought down his hand vigorously upon the table—"there has been prussic acid in the glass from which Mr. Benson drank this evening. The smell of bitter almonds is not to be mistaken."

An interval of silent horror followed this announcement, then a vehement "Great Heaven!" broke from the lips of Uncle Joe, while Hartley Benson, growing more and more rigid in his bearing, fixed his eyes on the doctor's face and barely ejaculated:

"Poison?"

"I say this," continued the doctor, too intent upon his own theory to notice either the growth of a terrible fear on the face of Uncle Joe, or the equally remarkable expression of subdued expectation on that of the son, "because long experience has taught me the uselessness of trying to hide such a fact as suicide, and also because, being the coroner of the county, it is my duty to warn you that an investigation will have to take place which will require certain precautions on my part, such as the sealing up of his papers, etc."

"That is true," came from the lips of both brother and son, over whom a visible change had passed at the word "suicide."

"But I cannot think—" the former began in an agitated voice.

"That my father would do such a deed," interposed the latter. "It does not seem probable, and yet he was a very wretched man, and grief will often drive the best of us to despair."

Uncle Joe gave his nephew a strange look, but said no more. The doctor went quietly on:

"I do not know what your father's troubles were, but that he committed suicide I greatly fear, unless it can be proved the acid was taken by mistake, a conclusion which does not seem probable, for from the smell of the decanter it is evident the acid was mixed with the wine, in which I now remember advising him to take the nightly powder I prescribed to him for quite a trivial disorder a few days ago. The only thing that puzzles me is, why, if he meditated death, he should have troubled himself to take this powder. And yet it is certain he did take it, for there is still some of the sediment of it remaining in the bottom of the glass."

"He took the powder because it was already in the glass," broke in Hartley, in a heavy tone of voice. "My sister put it there before she went up stairs to dress. I think she was afraid he would forget it. My father was very careless about small matters."

"He was careful enough not to poison any one else in the family," quoth the doctor. "There was scarcely a drop left in the decanter; he took the whole dose."

"I beg your pardon, sirs, but is it suicide you are talking about?" cried a voice suddenly over their shoulders, making them all start. Jonas, the servant, had entered from the inner room, and unseen by all but myself, had been listening to the last few words as if his life depended upon what they had to say. "If it is, why I have a bit of an observation of my own to make that may help you to settle the matter."

"You! What have you to say?" quoth the doctor, turning in surprise at the confident tone of voice in which the man spoke.

"Not much, I am sure," cried Hartley, to whom the appearance at that moment of his father's old servant was evidently most unwelcome.

"That is for you to judge, gentlemen. I can only tell you what I've seen, and that not ten minutes ago. Mr. Hartley, do you mind the man in the yellow dress that was flitting about the parlors all the evening?"

"Good heavens!" burst in uncontrollable agitation from Uncle Joe; and he caught his nephew by the arm with a look that called back the old rigid expression to the latter's face.

"Yes," was the quiet reply; "I remember seeing such a person."

"Well, sirs, I don't know as you will think any thing of it, but a little while ago I was walking up and down the balcony outside there, when I happened to look into this room, and I saw that man in the yellow dress leaning over this very table, looking into the wineglass Miss Carrie had put there for master. He had it in his hand, and his head was down very close to it, but what he did to it or to the decanter either, I am sure, sirs, I don't know, for I was that frightened at seeing this spectre in the room master had kept locked all day, that I just slipped off the balcony and ran round the house to find Mr. Hartley. But you wasn't in the parlors, sir, nor Miss Carrie neither, and when I got to this room, there was master lying dead on the floor, and everybody crowding around him horror-struck."

"Humph!" ejaculated the doctor, looking at Uncle Joe, who had sunk in a heap into the arm-chair his nephew abstractedly pushed toward him.

"You see, sirs," Jonas resumed, with great earnestness, "Mr. Benson, for some reason or other, had been very particular about keeping his own room to-day. The library door was locked as early as six this morning, and he would let no one in without first asking who was there. That's why I felt so dumbfoundered at seeing this yellow man in the room; besides—"

But no sooner had the good man arrived at this point than he stopped, with a gasp, and after a quick look at Hartley, flushed, and drew back in a state of great agitation and embarrassment. Evidently a suspicion had just crossed the mind of this old and attached servant as to whom the Yellow Domino might be.

"Well, well," cried the doctor, "go on; let us hear the rest."

"I—I have nothing more to say," mumbled the man, while Hartley, with an equal display of embarrassment, motioned the discomfited servant to withdraw, and turned as if to hide his face over some papers on the table.

"I think the man in the yellow domino had better be found," quoth the physician, dryly, glancing from Hartley to the departing form of the servant, with a sharp look. "At all events it would be well enough for us to know who he is."

"I don't see—" began Uncle Joe, but stopped as he perceived the face of Hartley Benson slowly composing itself. Evidently he was as much interested as myself in observing what this not-easily-to-be-understood man would say and do in this sudden crisis.

We were not long left in doubt.

"Doctor," he began, in a slow, hesitating tone, well calculated to produce the effect he desired, "we unfortunately already know who wore a yellow domino this evening. My brother Joe—"

"Hush!" implored his uncle, laying a hand on his nephew's arm with a quick look of distress not lost on the doctor.

"Brother?" repeated the latter. "Pardon me, I did not know—Ah, but I do remember now to have heard that Mr. Benson had another son."

The face of Hartley grew graver and graver. "My brother has been alienated from my father for some time, so you have never seen him here. But to-night he hoped, or made me think he hoped, to effect a reconciliation; so I managed, with my sister, to provide him with the domino necessary to insure him an entrance here. Indeed, I did more; I showed him a private door by which he could find his way into the library, never suspecting any harm could come of son and father meeting even in this surreptitious way. I—I loved my brother, and notwithstanding the past, had confidence in him. Nor can I think now he had any thing to do with the—" Here the voice of this inimitable actor broke in well-simulated distress. He sank on a chair and put his hands before his face.

The doctor had no reason to doubt this man. He therefore surveyed him with a look of grave regard.

"Mr. Benson," said he, "you have my profoundest sympathy. A tragedy like this in a family of such eminent respectability, is enough to overwhelm the stoutest heart. If your brother is here—"

"Dr. Travis," broke in the other, rising and grasping the physician's hand with an appearance of manly impulse impressive in one usually so stern and self contained, "you are, or were, my father's friend; can you or will you be ours? Dreadful as it is to think, my father undoubtedly committed suicide. He had a great dread of this day. It is the anniversary of an occurrence harrowing for him to remember. My brother—you see I shall have to break the secrecy of years—was detected by him in the act of robbing his desk three years ago to-night, and upon each and every recurrence of the day, has returned to his father's house to beg for the forgiveness and restoration to favor which he lost by that deed of crime. Hitherto my father has been able to escape his importunities, by absence or the address of his servants, but to-day he seemed to have a premonition that his children were in league against him, notwithstanding Carrie's ruse of the ball, and the knowledge may have worked upon him to that extent that he preferred death to a sight of the son that had ruined his life and made him the hermit you have seen."

The doctor fell into the trap laid for him with such diabolical art.

"Perhaps; but if that is so, why is your brother not here? Only a few minutes could have elapsed between the time that Jonas saw him leaning over the table with the glass in his hand and the moment when you and your sister entered this room in face of your father's falling form. He must have been present, therefore, when your father came from his bedroom, if not when he drank the fatal glass; why, then, did he take such pains to escape, if actuated by no keener emotion than horror at a father's suicide?"

"I do not know, I cannot say; but that he himself put the poison in the decanter I will not believe. A thief is not necessarily a parricide. Even if he were in great straits and needed the money my father's will undoubtedly leaves him, he would think twice before he ran the risk of making Carrie and myself his natural enemies. No, no, if my father has died from poison, it was through a mistake, or by the administration of his own hand, never by that of Joe Benson's."

"Ah, and has anybody here present dared to charge him with such a deed!"

With a start both gentlemen turned; an accusing spirit stood before them.

"Edith!" broke from Hartley's lips. "This is no place for you! Go back! go back!"

"My place is where the name of Joseph Benson is uttered," she proudly answered, "whether the words be for good or evil. I am his betrothed wife as you know, and again I ask, who has dared to utter an insinuation, however light, that he, the tender son and generous brother, has had a criminal hand in his father's awful death?"

"No one! no one!" essayed Hartley, taking her hand with a weak attempt at soothing. "I was but saying—"

But she turned from him with a gesture of repugnance, and taking a step toward the doctor, looked him entreatingly in the face. "You have not been expressing doubts of Mr. Benson's youngest son, because he happened to wear a disguise and be present when Mr. Benson fell? You do not know Joe, sir; nobody in this town knows him. His own father was ignorant of his worth; but we know him, Uncle Joe and I, and we know he could never do a deed that could stamp him either as a dishonorable or a criminal man. If Mr. Benson has died from poison, I should as soon think this man had a hand in it as his poor exiled brother." And in a burst of uncontrollable wrath and indignation, she pointed, with a sudden gesture, at the startled Hartley.

But that worthy, though evidently taken aback, was not to be caught so easily.

"Edith, you forget yourself," said he, with studied self-possession. "The horrors of this dreadful occurrence have upset you. I do not wonder at it myself, but the doctor will not so readily understand you. Miss Underhill has been strangely attached to my brother," he went on, turning to the latter with an apologetic smile that made Uncle Joe grind his teeth in silent wrath. "They were engaged previous to the affair of which I have just made mention, and naturally she could never bring herself to consider him guilty of a crime which, once acknowledged, must necessarily act as a bar of separation between them. She calls him a martyr, a victim, an exile, any thing but what he actually is. Indeed, she seems really to believe in his innocence, while we,"—he paused and looked up at his sister Carrie who had entered the room,—"while we," he went on slowly and sadly, taking this new ally softly by the hand, "know only too well that the unhappy boy was in every respect guilty of the crime for which his father exiled him. But that is neither here nor there; the dreadful subject before us is not what he once did, but whether his being here to-night has had any thing to do with my father's death. I cannot think it has, and yet—"

The subtle inflection of his voice spoke volumes. This great actor had evidently been driven to bay.

"O Hartley!" came in a terrified cry from his sister; "what is this? You cannot think, they cannot think, Joe could do any thing so dreadful as that?" while over the face of Edith passed a look of despair, as she saw the countenance of the doctor slowly fill with the gloom of suspicion, and even the faithful Uncle Joe turn away as if he too had been touched by the blight of a secret doubt.

"Ah, but I wish Joe were here himself!" she cried with startling emphasis. "He should speak, even if it brought ruin amongst us."

But the doctor was a man not to be moved by so simple a thing as a woman's unreasoning emotion.

"Yes, the Yellow Domino would be very welcome just now," he allowed, with grim decision.

"That he is not here is the most damning fact of all," Hartley slowly observed. "He fled when he saw our father fall."

"But he shall come back," Edith vehemently declared.

"If he does, I shall need no further proof of his innocence," said Uncle Joe.

"Nor I, so that he comes to-night," returned the doctor.

"Then be satisfied, for here he is," I exclaimed from my retreat; and drawing the mask over my face, and hastily enveloping myself in the yellow domino, I stepped forth into full view of the crowd around the table.

CHAPTER V

THE YELLOW DOMINO

A mingled sound of shrieks and exclamations greeted me.

"Joe!" cried Edith, bounding forward.

But I waved her back, and turned with a severe gesture toward Hartley Benson.

"What are your reasons," I demanded, "for thinking the poisoning that has taken place here was the work of the Yellow Domino?"

"Do you ask me?" he retorted, after a moment's pause, during which my voice echoed through the room, waking strange gleams of doubt on the faces of more than one person present. "You wish to dare me, then?" he hissed, coming a step nearer.

"I wish to know what the Yellow Domino has done that you or any one should consider him as responsible for the tragedy that has here taken place," I steadily replied.

"Are you not my brother, then?" he cried, in mingled rage and anxiety. "Was it not you I met under the evergreens and supplied with a yellow domino, in order to give you the opportunity of seeing our father to-night and effecting the reconciliation which you had so long desired? Are you not he who afterward followed me to this room and hid himself in the closet from which you have just come, all for the purpose, as you said, of throwing yourself at your father's feet and begging pardon for a past of which you had long ago repented? Or are you some reckless buffoon who has presumed to step into the domino my brother left behind him, and careless of the terrible trouble that has overwhelmed this family, come here with your criminal jests to puzzle and alarm us?"

"I am the man to whom you gave the domino, if that is what you wish to know, Hartley Benson; and I am the man whom you led into the ambush of this closet, for such reasons as your own conscience must inform you. If the Yellow Domino put poison into Mr. Benson's wine, then upon me must lie the burden of the consequences, for I alone have worn the disguise of this mask from the moment we met under the evergreens till now, as I think may be proved by this gentleman you call Uncle Joe, and this lady you address as Edith."

This mode of attack had the desired effect.

"Who are you?" burst from Hartley's lips, now blanched to the color of clay. "Unmask him, doctor; let us see the man who dares to play us tricks on such a night as this!"

"Wait!" cried I, motioning back not only the doctor, but Uncle Joe and the ladies—the whole group having started forward at Hartley's words. "Let us first make sure I am the Yellow Domino who has been paraded through the parlors this evening. Miss Benson, will you pardon me if I presume to ask you what were the words of salutation with which you greeted me to-night?"

"Oh!" she cried, in a tremble of doubt and dismay, "I do not know as I can remember; something about being glad to see you, I believe, and my hope that your plans for the evening might succeed."

"To which," said I, "I made no audible reply, but pressed your hand in mine, with the certainty you were a friend though you had not used the word 'Counterfeit.'"

"Yes, yes," she returned, blushing and wildly disturbed, as she had reason to be.

"And you, Uncle Joe," I went on; "what were your words? How did you greet the man you had been told was your erring nephew?"

"I said: 'To counterfeit wrong when one is right, necessarily opens one to a misunderstanding.'"

"To which ambiguous phrase I answered, as you will remember, with a simple, 'That is true,' a reply by the way that seemed to arouse your curiosity and lead to strange revelations."

"God defend us!" cried Uncle Joe.

The exclamation was enough. I turned to the trembling Edith.

"I shall not attempt," said I, "to repeat or ask you to repeat any conversation which may have passed between us, for you will remember it was too quickly interrupted by Mr. Benson for us to succeed in uttering more than a dozen or so words. However, you will do me the kindness to acknowledge your belief that I am the man who stood with you behind the parlor curtains an hour ago."

"I will," she replied, with a haughty lift of her head that spoke more loudly than her blushes.

"It only remains, then, for Mr. Benson to assure himself I am the person who followed him to the closet. I know of no better way of his doing this than to ask him if he remembers the injunctions which he was pleased to give me, when he bestowed upon me this domino."

"No,—that is,—whatever they were, they were given to the man I supposed to be my brother."

"Ha, then; it was to your brother," I rejoined, "you gave that hint about the glass I would find on the library table; saying that if it did not smell of wine I would know your father had not had his nightly potion and would yet come to the library to drink it;—an intimation, as all will acknowledge, which could have but the one result of leading me to go to the table and take up the glass and look into it in the suspicious manner which has been reported to you."

He was caught in his own toils and saw it. Muttering a deep curse, he drew back, while a startled "Humph!" broke from the doctor, followed by a quick, "Is that true? Did you tell him that, Mr. Benson?"

For reply the now thoroughly alarmed villain leaped at my throat. "Off with that toggery! Let us see your face! I shall and will know who you are."

But I resisted for another moment while I added: "It is, then, established to your satisfaction that I am really the man who has worn the yellow domino this evening. Very well, now look at me, one and all, and say if you think I am likely to be a person to destroy Mr. Benson." And with a quick gesture I threw aside my mask, and yielded the fatal yellow domino to the impatient hands of Mr. Hartley Benson.

The result was a cry of astonishment from those to whom the face thus revealed was a strange one, and a curse deep and loud from him to whom the shock of that moment's surprise must have been nearly overwhelming.

"Villain!" he shrieked, losing his self-possession in a sudden burst of fury; "spy! informer! I understand it all now. You have been set over me by my brother. Instructed by him, you have dared to enter this house, worm yourself into its secrets, and by a deviltry only equalled by your presumption, taken advantage of your position to poison my father and fling the dreadful consequences of your crime in the faces of his mourning family. It was a plot well laid; but it is foiled, sir, foiled, as you will see when I have you committed to prison to-morrow."

"Mr. Benson," I returned, shaking him loose as I would a feather, "this is all very well; but in your haste and surprise you have made a slight mistake. You call me a spy; so I am; but a spy backed by the United States Government is not a man to be put lightly into prison. I am a detective, sir, connected at present with the Secret Service at Washington. My business is to ferret out crime and recognize a rogue under any disguise and in the exercise of any vile or deceptive practices." And I looked him steadily in the face.

Then indeed his cheek turned livid, and the eye which had hitherto preserved its steadiness sought the floor.

"A detective!" murmured Miss Carrie, shrinking back from the cringing form of the brother whom, but a few hours before, she had deemed every thing that was noble and kind.

"A detective!" echoed Edith, brightening like a rose in the sunshine.

"In government employ!" repeated Uncle Joe, honoring me with a stare that was almost comic in its mingled awe and surprise.

"Yes," I rejoined; "if any one doubts me, I have papers with me to establish my identity. By what means I find myself in this place, a witness of Mr. Benson's death and the repository of certain family secrets, it is not necessary for me to inform you. It is enough that I am here, have been here for a good hour, posted behind that curtain; that I heard Jonas' exclamation as he withdrew from the balcony, saw Mr. Benson come in from his bedroom, drink his glass of wine, and afterward fall at the feet of his son and daughter; and that having been here, and the witness of all this, I can swear that if Mr. Benson drank poison from yonder decanter, he drank poison that was put into it before either he or the Yellow Domino entered this room. Who put it there, it is for you to determine; my duty is done for to-night." And with a bow I withdrew from the group about me and crossed to the door.

But Miss Carrie's voice, rising in mingled shame and appeal, stopped me. "Don't go," said she; "not at least until you tell me where my brother Joseph is. Is he in this town, or has he planned this deception from a distance? I—I am an orphan, sir, who at one blow has lost not only a dearly beloved father but, as I fear, a brother too, in whom, up to this hour, I have had every confidence. Tell me, then, if any support is left for a most unhappy girl, or whether I must give up all hopes of even my brother Joe's sympathy and protection."

"Your brother Joe," I replied, "has had nothing to do with my appearance here. He and I are perfect strangers; but if he is a tall, broad-shouldered, young man, shaped something like myself, but with a ruddy cheek and light curling hair, I can tell you I saw such a person enter the shrubbery at the southwest corner of the garden an hour or so ago."

"No, he is here!" came in startling accents over my shoulders. And with a quick leap Joe Benson sprang by me and stood handsome, tall, and commanding in the centre of the room. "Hartley! Carrie! Edith! what is this I hear? My father stricken down, my father dying or dead, and I left to wander up and down through the shrubbery, while you knelt at his bedside and received his parting blessing? Is this the recompense you promised me, Hartley? this your sisterly devotion, Carrie? this your love and attention to my interests, Edith?"

"O Joe, dear Joe, do not blame us!" Carrie made haste to reply. "We thought you were here. A man was here, that man behind you, simulating you in every regard, and to him we gave the domino, and from him we have learned—"

"What?" sprang in thundering tones from the young giant's throat as he wheeled on his heel and confronted me.

"That your brother Hartley is a villain," I declared, looking him steadily in the eye.

"God!" was his only exclamation as he turned slowly back and glanced toward his trembling brother.

"Sir," said I, taking a step toward Uncle Joe, who, between his eagerness to embrace the new-comer and his dread of the consequences of this unexpected meeting, stood oscillating from one side to the other in a manner ridiculous enough to see, "what do you think of the propriety of uttering aloud and here, the suspicions which you were good enough to whisper into my ears an hour ago? Do you see any reason for altering your opinion as to which of the two sons of Mr. Benson invaded his desk and appropriated the bonds afterward found in their common apartment, when you survey the downfallen crest of the one and compare it with the unfaltering look of the other?"

"No," he returned, roused into sudden energy by the start given by Hartley. And advancing between the brothers, he looked first at one and then at the other with a long, solemn gaze that called out the color on Hartley's pale cheek and made the crest of Joe rise still higher in manly pride and assertion. "Joe," said he, "for three years now your life has lain under a shadow. Accused by your father of a dreadful crime, you have resolutely refused to exonerate yourself, notwithstanding the fact that a dear young girl waited patiently for the establishment of your innocence in order to marry you. To your family this silence meant guilt, but to me and mine it has told only a tale of self-renunciation and devotion. Joe, was I right in this? was Edith right? The father you so loved, and feared to grieve, is dead. Speak, then: Did you or did you not take the bonds that were found in the cupboard at the head of your bed three years ago to-night? The future welfare, not only of this faithful child but of the helpless sister, who, despite her belief in your guilt, has clung to you with unwavering devotion, depends upon your reply."

"Let my brother speak," was the young man's answer, given in a steady and nobly restrained tone.

"Your brother will not speak," his uncle returned. "Don't you see you must answer for yourself? Say, then: Are you the guilty man your father thought you, or are you not? Let us hear, Joe."

"I am not!" avowed the young man, bowing his head in a sort of noble shame that must have sent a pang of anguish through the heart of his brother.

"Oh, I knew it, I knew it!" came from Edith's lips in a joyous cry, as she bounded to his side and seized him by one hand, just as his sister grasped the other in a burst of shame and contrition that showed how far she was removed from any participation in the evil machinations of her elder brother.

The sight seemed to goad Hartley Benson to madness. Looking from one to the other, he uttered a cry that yet rings in my memory: "Carrie! Edith! do you both forsake me, and all because of a word which any villain might have uttered? Is this the truth and constancy of women? Is this what I had a right to expect from a sister, a—a friend? Carrie, you at least always gave me your trust,—will you take it away because a juggling spy and a recreant brother have combined to destroy me?"

But beyond a wistful look and a solemn shake of the head, Carrie made no response, while Edith, with her eyes fixed on the agitated countenance of her lover, did not even seem to hear the words of pleading that were addressed to her.

The shock of the disappointment was too much for Hartley Benson. Clenching his hand upon his breast, he gave one groan of anguish and despair and sank into a chair, inert and helpless. But before we could any of us take a step toward him, before the eyes of the doctor and mine could meet in mutual understanding, he had bounded again to his feet, and in a burst of desperation seized the chair in which he sat, and held it high above his head.

"Fools! dotards!" he exclaimed, his eyes rolling in frenzy from face to face, but lingering longest on mine, as if there he read the true secret of his overthrow, as well as the promise of his future doom. "You think it is all over with me; that there is nothing left for you to do but to stand still and watch how I take my defeat. But I am a man who never acknowledges defeat. There is still a word I have to say that will make things a little more even between us. Listen for it, you. It will not be long in coming, and when you hear it, let my brother declare how much enjoyment he will ever get out of his victory."

And whirling the chair about his head, he plunged through our midst into the hall without.

For an instant we stood stupefied, then Carrie Benson's voice rose in one long, thrilling cry, and with a bound she rushed toward the door. I put out my hand to stop her, but it was not necessary. Before she could cross the threshold the sudden, sharp detonation of a pistol-shot was heard in the hall, and we knew that the last dreadful word of that night's tragedy had been spoken.

The true secret of Hartley Benson's action in this matter was never discovered. That he planned his father's violent death, no one who was present at the above interview ever doubted. That he went further than that, and laid his plans in such a manner that the blame, if blame ensued, should fall upon his innocent brother, was equally plain, especially after the acknowledgment we received from Jonas, that he went out on the balcony and looked in the window at the special instigation of his young master. But why this arch villain, either at his own risk or at that of the man he hated, felt himself driven to such a revolting crime, will never be known; unless, indeed, the solution be found in his undoubted passion for the beautiful Edith, and in the accumulated pressure of certain secret debts for whose liquidation he dared not apply to his father.

I never revealed to this family the true nature of the motives which actuated me in my performance of the part I played that fatal night. It was supposed by Miss Carrie and the rest, that I was but obeying instructions given me by Mr. Benson; and I never undeceived them. I was too much ashamed of the curiosity which was the mainspring of my action to publish each and every particular of my conduct abroad; though I could not but congratulate myself upon its results when, some time afterward, I read of the marriage of Joe and Edith.

The counterfeiters were discovered and taken, but not by me.

THREE THOUSAND DOLLARS

CHAPTER I

"Do You Know What Would Happen to Him?"

"Now state your problem."

The man who was thus addressed shifted uneasily on the long bench which he and his companion bestrode. He was facing the speaker, and though very little light sifted through the cobweb-covered window high over their heads, he realized that what there was fell on his features, and he was not sure of his features, or of what effect their expression might have on the other man.

"Are you sure we are quite alone in this big, desolate place?" he asked.

It seemed a needless question. Though it was broad daylight outside and they were in the very heart of the most populated district of lower New York, they could not have been more isolated had the surrounding walls been those of some old ruin in the heart of an untraversed desert.

A short description of the place will explain this. They were in the forsaken old church not far from Avenue A—, a building long given over to desolation, and empty of everything but débris and one or two broken stalls, which for some inscrutable reason—possibly from some latent instinct of inherited reverence—had not yet been converted into junk and sold to the old clothes men by the rapacious denizens of the surrounding tenements.

Perhaps you remember this building; perhaps some echo of the bygone and romantic has come to you as you passed its decaying walls once dedicated to worship, but soulless now and only distinguishable from the five-story tenements pressing up on either side, by its one high window in which some bits of colored glass still lingered amid its twisted and battered network. You may remember the building and you may remember the stray glimpses afforded you through the arched opening in the lower story of one of the adjacent tenements, of the churchyard in its rear with its chipped and tumbling head-*stones just showing here and there above the accumulated litter. But it is not probable that you have any recollections of the interior of the church itself, shut as it has been from the eye of the public for nearly a generation. And it is with the interior we have to do—a great hollow vault where once altar and priest confronted a reverent congregation. There is no altar here now, nor any chancel; hardly any floor. The timbers which held the pews have rotted and fallen away, and what was once a cellar has received all this rubbish and held it piled up in mounds which have blocked up most of the windows and robbed the place even of the dim religious light which was once its glory, so that when the man whose words we have just quoted asked if they were quite alone and peered into the dim, belumbered corners, it was but natural for his hardy, resolute, and unscrupulous companion to snort with impatience and disgust as he answered:

"Would I have brought you here if I hadn't known it was the safest place in New York for this kind of talk? Why, man, there may be in this city five men all told, who know the trick of the door I unfastened for you, and not one of them is a cop. You may take my word for that. Besides—"

"But the kids? They're everywhere; and if one of them should have followed us—"

"Do you know what would happen to him? I'll tell you a story—no, I won't; you're frightened enough already. But there's no kid here, nor any one else but our two selves, unless it be some wandering spook from the congregations laid outside; and spooks don't count. So out with your proposition, Mr. Fellows. I—"

CHAPTER II

"Thousands in That Safe"

"No names!" hoarsely interrupted the other. "If you speak my name again I'll give the whole thing up."

"No you won't; you're too deep in it for that. But I'll drop the Fellows and just call you Sam. If that's too familiar, we'll drop the job. I'm not so keen on it."

"You will be. It's right in your line." Sam Fellows, as he was called, was whispering now—a hot, eager whisper, breathing of guilt and desperation. "If I could do it alone—but I haven't the wit—the—"

"Experience," dryly put in the other. "Well, well!" he exclaimed impatiently, as Fellows crept nearer, but said nothing.

"I'm going to speak, but—Well, then, here's how it is!" he suddenly conceded, warned by the other's eye. "The building is a twenty-story one, chuck full and alive with business. The room I mean is on the twelfth floor; it is one of five, all communicating, and all in constant use except the one holding the safe. And that is visited constantly. Some one is always going in and out. Indeed, it is a rule of the firm that every one of the employees must go into that room once, at least, during the day, and remain there for five minutes alone. I do it; every one does it; it's a very mysterious proceeding which only a crank like my employer would devise."

"What do you do there?"

"Nothing. I'm speaking now for myself. The others—some of the others—one of the others may open the safe. That's what I believe, that's what I want to know about and how it's done. There are thousands in that safe, and the old man being away—"

"Yes, this is all very interesting. Go on. What you want is an artist with a jimmy."

"No, no. It's no such job as that. I want to know the person, the trusted person who has all those securities within touch. It's a mania with me. I should have been the man. I'm—I'm manager."

The hoarseness with which this word was uttered, the instinct of shame which made his eyes fall as it struggled from his lips, wakened a curious little gleam of hardy cynicism in the steady gaze of his listener.

"Oh, you're manager, are you!" came in slow retort, filling a silence that had more of pain than pleasure in it. "Well, manager, your story is very interesting, but by no means complete. Suppose you hurry on to the next instalment."

Cringing as from a blow, Fellows took up his tale, no longer creeping nearer his would-be confederate, but, if anything, edging away.

CHAPTER III

"How Does it Stand"

"I've watched and watched and watched," said he, "but I can't pick out the man. Letters come, orders are given, and those orders are carried out, but not by me. I'm speaking now of investments, or the payment of large sums; anything which calls for the opening of that safe where the old man has stuffed away his thousands. Small matters fall to my share. There is another safe, of which I hold the combination. Child's play, but the other! It would make both of us independent, and yet leave something for appearances. But it can't be worked. It stands in front of a glass door from which the curtain is drawn every night. Every passerby can look in. If it is opened it must be done in broad daylight and by the person whom the old man trusts. By that means only would I get my revenge, and revenge is what I want. He don't trust me, me who have been with him for seven years and—"

"Drop that, it isn't interesting. The facts are what I want. What kind of safe is it?"

"The strangest you ever saw. I don't know who made it. There's nothing on it to show. Nor is there a lock or combination. But it opens. You can just see the outline of a door. Steel—fine steel, and not so very large, but the contents—"

"We'll take its contents for granted. How does it stand? On a platform?"

"Yes, one foot from the floor. The platform runs all the way across the room and holds other things; a table which nobody uses, a revolving bookcase and a series of shelves, fitted with boxes containing old receipts and such junk. Sometimes I go through these; but nothing ever comes of it." He paused, as if the subject were distasteful.

"And the safe is opened?"

"Almost every week. I'm ashamed to tell you the old duffer's methods; they're loony. But he isn't a lunatic. At any rate, they don't think so in Wall Street."

"I'll make a guess at his name."

"Not yet. You'll have to swear—"

"Oh, we're both in it. Never mind the heroics. It's too good a thing to peach on. Me and the manager! I like that. Take it easy till the job's done, anyway. And now I'll take a fly at the name. It's—"

He had the grace to whisper.

CHAPTER IV

"Stenographers Must Be Counted"

Young Fellows squirmed and turned a shade paler, if one could trust the sickly violet ray that shot down from the once exquisitely colored window high up over their heads.

"Hush!" he muttered; and the other grinned. Evidently the guess was a correct one.

"No, he's no lunatic," the professional quietly declared. "But he has queer ways. Which of his queers do you object to?"

"When his letters come, or more often his cablegrams, they are opened by me and then put in plain view on a certain little bulletin board in the main office. These are his orders. Any one who knows the cipher can read them. I don't know the cipher. At night I take them down, number them, and file them away. They have served their purpose. They have been seen by the person whose business it is to carry out his instructions, and the rest you must guess. His brokers know the secret, but it is never discussed by us. The least word and the next cablegram would read in good plain English, 'Fire him!' I've had that experience. I've had to fire three since he went away two months ago."

"That's good."

"Why good?"

"That cuts out three from your list. The person is not among the ones dismissed."

"That's so." New life seemed to spring up in Fellows. "You'll do the job," he cried. "Somehow, I never thought of going about it that way. And I know another man that's out."

"Who?"

"Myself, for one. There are only seven more."

"Counting all?"

"All."

"Stenographers included?"

"Oh, stenographers!"

"Stenographers must be counted."

"Well, then, seven men and one woman. Our stenographer is a woman."

"What kind of a woman?"

"A young girl. Ordinary, but good enough. I've never noticed her very much."

"Tell me about the men."

"What's the use? You wouldn't take my word. They're a cheap lot, beneath contempt in my estimation. There's not one of them clever enough for the business. Jack Forbush comes the nearest to it, and probably is the one. The way he keeps his eye on me makes me suspect him. Or is he, too, playing my game?"

"How can I tell? How can I tell anything from what you say? I'll have to look into the matter myself. Give me the names and addresses and I'll look the parties up. Get their rating, so to speak. Leave it to me, and I'll land the old man's confidential clerk."

"Here's the list. I thought you might want it."

"Where's the girl's name?"

"The girl! Oh, pshaw!"

"Put her name down just the same."

"There, then. Grace Lee. Address, 74 East — Street. And now swear on the honor of a gentleman—"

Beau Johnson pulled the rim of Fellows's hat over his eyes to suggest what he thought of this demand.

CHAPTER V

"I've Business with Him"

Next day there appeared at the offices of Thomas Stoughton, in Nassau Street, a trim, well-looking man, who had urgent business with Mr. Fellows, the manager. He was kept waiting for some time before being introduced into that gentleman's private room; but this did not seem to disturb him. There was plenty to look at, or so he seemed to think, and his keen, noncommittal eyes flashed hither and thither and from face to face with restless activity. He seemed particularly interested in the bookkeeper of the establishment, but it was an interest which did not last long, and when a neat, pleasant-faced young woman rose from her seat and passed rapidly across the room, it was upon her his eyes settled and remained fixed, with a growing attention, until a certain door closed upon her with a sound like a snapping lock. Then he transferred his attention to the door, and was still gazing at it when a boy summoned him to the manager's office.

He went in with reluctance. He had rather have watched that door. But he had questions to ask, and so made a virtue of necessity. Mr. Fellows was not pleased to see him. He started quite guiltily from his seat and only sat again on compulsion—the compulsion of his visitor's steady and quelling eye.

"I've business with you, Mr. Fellows." Then, the boy being gone, "Which is the room? The one opening out of the general office directly opposite this?"

Mr. Fellows nodded.

"I have just seen one of the employees go in there. I should like to see that person come out. Do you mind talking with this door open? I know enough about banking to hold up my end of the conversation."

Fellows rose with a jerk and pushed the door back. His visitor smiled easily and launched into a discussion about stocks and bonds interspersed with a few assertions and questions not meant for the general ear, as:

"It's the girl who is in there. Not ordinary, by any means. Just the sort an old smudge like Stoughton would be apt to trust. Now what's that?"

"Singing. She often sings. I've forbidden it, but she forgets, she says," answered Fellows.

"Pretty good music. Listen to that note. High as a prima donna's. Does she sing at her work?"

"No; I'd fire her if she did. It's only when she's walking about or when—"

"She's in that room?"

"Yes."

"At par? I buy nothing at par. There! She's coming. I wish I dared intercept her, rifle her pockets. Do you know if she has pockets?"

"No; how should I?"

"Fellows, you're not worth your salt. Ah! there's a face for you, and I can read it like a book. Did a letter or cablegram come to-day?"

"Yes; didn't you see it? Hung up in the outer office."

"I thought I saw something. Ninety-five? That's a quotation worth listening to. Three at ninety-five. That girl's a trump. I will see more of my lady." Here he took care to shut the door. "I've been the rounds, Fellows. Private-detective work and all that. She is the only puzzler among the group. You'll hear from me again; meanwhile treat the girl well. Don't spring any traps; leave that to me."

And Fellows, panting with excitement, promised, muttering under his breath:

"A woman! That's even worse than I thought. But we'll make the old fellow pay for it. Those securities are ours. I already feel them in my hand."

The sinister twitch which marred the other's mouth emphasized the assertion in a way Grace Lee's friends would have trembled to see.

CHAPTER VI

That evening a young woman and a young man sat on one of the benches in Central Park. They were holding hands, but modestly and with a clinging affection. No one appeared in sight; they had the moonlight, the fragrance of the spring foliage, and their true love all to themselves. The woman was Grace, the young man was Philip Andrews, a candid-eyed, whole-hearted fellow whom any girl might be proud to be seen with, much more to be engaged to. Grace was proud, but she was more than that; her heart was all involved in her hope—a good heart which he was equally proud to have won. Yet while love was theirs and the surroundings breathed peace and joy, they did not look quite happy. A cloud was on his brow and something like a tear in her eye as she spoke gently but with rare firmness.

"Philip, we must wait. One love does not put out another. I cannot leave my old father now. He is too feeble and much too dependent on me. Philip, you do not know my father. You have seen him, it is true, many, many times. You have talked with him and even have nursed him at odd moments, when I had to be out of the room getting supper or supplying some of his many wants. Yet you do not know him."

"I know that he is intelligent."

"Yes, yes, that is evident. Any one can see that. And you can see, too, that he is frequently fretful and exacting, as all old people are. But the qualities he shows me—his strong, melancholy, but devoted nature, quickened by an unusually unhappy life—that you do not see and cannot, much as you like him and much as he likes you. Only the child who has surprised him at odd moments, when he thought himself quite alone, wringing his hands and weeping over some intolerable memory—who has listened in the dead of night to his smothered but heart-breaking groans, can know either his suffering or the one joy which palliates it. If I could tell you his story—but that would be treason to one whose rights I am bound to reverence. You will respect my silence, but you must also take my word that he needs and has a right to all the pleasure and all the hope my love can give him. I cannot be with him much; my work forbids, but the little time I have is his, except on rare occasions like this, and he knows it and is satisfied. Were I married—. But you will wait, Philip. It may not be long—he grows weaker every day. Besides, you are not ready yet yourself. You are doing wonderfully well, but a year's freedom will help you materially, as it will me. Every day is adding to our store; in a year we may be almost independent."

"Grace, you have misunderstood me. I said that I was no good without you, that I needed your presence to make a man of me, but I did not mean that you were to share my fortunes now. I would not ask that. I would be a fool or worse, for, Grace, I'm not doing so well as you think. While I knew that my present employment was for a specified time, I had hopes of continuing on. But this cannot be. That's what I have to tell you to-night. It looks as if our marriage would have to be postponed indefinitely instead of hastened. And I can't bear it. You don't know what you are to me, or what this disappointment is. I expected to be raised, not dismissed, and if I had had—"

"What?"

The word came very softly, and with rare tenderness. It made him turn and look at her sweet, upturned face, with its resources of strength and shy, unfathomable smile. "What?" she asked again, with a closer pressure of her hand. "You must finish all your sentences with me."

"I'm ashamed." He uttered it breathlessly. "What am I, to say, 'If I had three thousand dollars the Stickney Company would keep me?' I have barely three hundred and those are dedicated to you."

CHAPTER VII

"I'm Sure That I Can Get Them For You"

"If you had three thousand!" She repeated it in surprise and yet with an indescribable air, which to one versed in human nature would have caught the attention and aroused strange inner inquiries. "Does the Stickney Company want money so badly as that?"

"That's not it. They have plainly told me that for three thousand dollars and my services they would give me ten thousand dollars' stock interest, but insist that the man who assumes the responsibility of the position must be financially interested as well. But I haven't the money, and without the money my experience appears to them valueless. I despair of getting another situation in these hard times and—Grace, you don't look sorry."

"Because—" she paused, and her fine eyes roamed about her jealous of a listener to her secret, but did not pierce the bush which rose up, cloudy with blossoms, a few feet behind their bench—"because it is not impossible for you to hope for those thousands. I think—I am sure that I can get them for you."

Her voice had sunk to a whisper, but it was a very clear whisper.

Young Andrews looked at her in surprise; there was something besides pleasure in that surprise.

"Where?" he asked.

She hesitated, and just at that moment the moon slipped behind a cloud.

"Where, Grace, can you get three thousand dollars? From Mr. Stoughton? He is generous to you, he pays you well for what you do for him, but I do not think he would give you that amount, nor do I think he would risk it on any venture involving my judgment. I should not like to have you ask him. I should like to rise feeling absolutely independent of Mr. Stoughton."

"I never thought of asking him. There is another way. I'd—I'd like to think it over. If your scheme is good—very good, I might be brought to aid you in the way my mind suggests. But I should want to be sure."

She was not looking at him now. If she had been, she might have been startled at his expression. Nor could he see her face; she had turned it aside.

"Grace," he prayed, "don't do anything rash. You handle so much money that three thousand dollars may seem very little to you. But it's a goodly sum to get or to replace if one loses it. You must not borrow—"

"I will not borrow."

"Nor raise it in any way without telling me the sacrifice you must make to obtain it. But it's all a dream; tell me that it's all a dream; you were talking from your wishes, not from any certainty you have. Say so, and I will not be disappointed. I do not want your money; I'd rather go poor and wait till the times change. Don't you see? I'd be more of a man."

"But you'd have to take it if I gave it to you, and—perhaps I shall. I want to see you happy, Philip; I must see you happy. I'd be willing to risk a good deal for that. I'm not so happy myself, father suffers so, and the care of it weighs on me. You are all I have to make me glad, and when you are troubled my heart goes down, down. But it's getting late, dear. It's time we went home. Don't ask me what's in my mind, but dream of riches. I'm sure they will come. You shall earn them with the three thousand dollars you want and which I will give you."

"I shall earn them honestly," were the last words he said, as they rose from the seat and began to move toward the gate. And the moon, coming out from its temporary eclipse, shone on his clear-cut face as he said this, but not on her bowed head and sidelong look. They were in the shadow.

There was something else in the shadow. As they moved away and disappeared in the darkness the long, slim figure of a man rose from behind the bush I have mentioned. He had a sparkling eye and a thin-lipped mouth, and he smiled very curiously as he looked after the pair before turning himself about and going the other way.

It was not Fellows; it was his chosen confederate in the nefarious scheme they had planned between them.

CHAPTER VIII

"I Did As You Bid Me"

Another meeting in the old church, but this time at night. The somberness of the surroundings was undiminished by any light. They were in absolute darkness. Absolute darkness, but not absolute silence. Noises strange and suggestive, but not of any human agency, whispered, sighed, rattled, and grumbled from far away recesses. The snap of wood, the gnawing of rats, the rustling of bat wings disturbed the ears of one of the guilty pair, till his voice took on unnatural tones as he tried to tell his story to his greedy companion. They were again astride the bench, and their thin faces were so near that their breaths commingled at times; yet Fellows felt at moments so doubtful of all human presence that instinctively his hand would go groping out till it touched the other's arm or breast, when it would fall back again satisfied. He was in a state of absolute terror of the darkness, the oppressive air, the ghostly sounds, and possibly of the image raised by his own conscience, yet he hugged to himself the thought of secrecy which it all involved, and never thought of yielding up his scheme or even shortening his tale, so long as the other listened and gave his mind to the problem which promised them thousands without the usual humdrum method of working for them.

We will listen to what he had to say, leaving to your imagination the breaks and guilty starts and moments of intense listening and anxious fear with which he seasoned it.

"I did as you bid me," he whispered. "Yesterday fresh orders came from abroad, in cipher, as usual. (It's an unreadable cipher. I've had experts on it many times.) I had hung it up, and though business was heavy, my business, you know, I had eyes for our fair friend, and knew every step she took about the offices. I even knew when her eyes first fell on the cablegram. I had my door open, and I caught her looking up from her work, and what was more, caught the pause in the click-click of the typewriter as she looked and read. If she had not been able to read, the click-click would have gone on, for I believe she could work that typewriter with her eyes shut. But her attention was caught, and she stopped. I tell you I've been humiliated for the last time. I'm in for anything that will make that girl step down and out. What was that!"

Muttered curses from his companion brought him back to his story. With a gulp he went on:

"You may bet your bottom dollar that I watched her after that, and sure enough, in less than half an hour she had gone into the room where the safe is. Instantly I prepared my coup d'état. I waited just long enough to hear her voice in that one song she sings, then I jumped from my seat and rushed to the door, shouting, 'Miss Lee! Miss Lee! Your father! Your father!' making hullabaloo enough to raise the dead and scare her out of her wits; for she dotes on that old man and would sell her soul for his sake, I do believe.

"Great heavens, it worked! As I live, it worked. I heard her voice fail on that high upper note of hers, and then the sound of her feet staggering, slipping over the floor, and in another moment the fumbling of her hand on the knob and the slow opening of the door which she seemed to have no power to manage. Helping her, I pulled it open, and there beyond her and her white, shocked face, I saw—I saw—"

CHAPTER IX

"'The Safe Door is Opened,' I Cried"

"Go on! Don't be a fool; that was nothing."

"I don't know; it was like a great sigh at my ear. But this is awful! Couldn't we have one spark of light?"

"And have the police upon us the next minute? Look up at that window. You can see it, can't you?"

"Yes, yes, but very faintly," Fellows whispered.

"But you can see it. So could those outside, if we had one glimmer of light in here. No, no, you'll have to stand the dark or quit. But you shan't quit till you've told me what you saw in the room where the safe is."

"The safe door opening." His voice trembled so that the other shook him to steady his nerves. "Not opened, mind you, but opening. It was like magic, and I stared so that she forgot her fears and forgot her questions. Turning from me with a startled cry, she looked behind her, and saw what I saw, and tried to push me out. 'I'll come, I'll come,' she whispered. 'Leave me a minute and I'll come.'

"But I wasn't going to do that. 'The safe door is opened,' I cried. 'Did you do it?' She didn't know what to say. I have never seen a woman in such a state; then she whispered in awful agitation, 'Yes; I've been given the combination by Mr. Stoughton. I'm duly following his orders. But my father! What about my father? You frightened me so I forgot that—' I waited, staring at her, but she didn't finish. She just asked, 'My father? What has happened to him?' 'Nothing serious,' I managed to say. I wished the old father was in ballyhack. But he'd served his turn; I must say that he'd served his turn. 'A telephone message,' I went on. 'He had had a nervous spell and wanted you. I said that you could go home at noon.' She stood looking at me doubtfully; then her eyes stole back to the safe. 'You will have to leave me here for a few minutes,' she said. 'I have Mr. Stoughton's business to attend to. He will not be pleased at my having given away his secret. He did not wish it known who controlled his affairs in his absence, but now that you do know, you will be doing the right thing to let me go on in the way he has planned for me. His orders must be carried out.'

"She is very determined, and understands herself only too well, but I am manager, and I paid her back in her own coin. 'That's all very well,' said I, 'but what proof have I that you are telling me the truth? You have opened the safe—you say you have the combination—but people sometimes surprise a combination and open a safe from other interests than those of their employer. You seem a good girl, but you are a girl, and there are men here much more likely to be in Mr. Stoughton's confidence than yourself. With that open safe before us I cannot leave you here alone. What you take from it I must see, and if possible be present at your negotiations. That I consider a manager's duty under the circumstances.' 'Mr. Fellows,' she asked, 'can you read this morning's telegram?' 'No,' I felt bound to reply. 'Then that acquits you. I can.' And again she tried to urge me to go out. But I would not be urged. I was staring across the room at the open safe and in fancy clutching its contents. In fact, I made one step toward them. But she drew herself up with such an air that I paused. She's a big girl, you know, and not to be fooled with when she's angry. 'Come a step farther and I will scream for the watchman,' she whispered. All our talk had been low, for there were listening ears everywhere—we couldn't risk that, and I stepped back. Immediately she saw her advantage, and added, 'If you do not think better of it and leave the room, I'll scream.' For answer to this I said that I—"

CHAPTER X

"I Have a Scheme"

"What?"

A yell answered him.

"Something hit me! Something hit me!"

"Yes, I hit you; and I'll hit you again if you don't go on."

Fellows shivered, attempted some puerile protest, balked, and stammeringly obeyed his restless and irritated companion.

"I—I said—I wasn't such a fool then as I am now—that she had lied when she told me that she had the combination. There was no combination. The safe did not even have a lock. The door opened with a spring. How had she induced that spring to give way? I demanded to know."

"And did she tell you?"

"No. She merely repeated, 'I will scream, and that will cause a scandal which will lead to your discharge, not mine.' So—so, I came out."

"Blast your eyes! And when did she come out?"

"Within five minutes. I watched the clock."

"And what did she have?"

"Nothing in sight."

"I see. A deep game. But I know a deeper. There is no possibility of breaking into that safe by night, undetected by the watchman?"

"None; and that watchman is incorruptible. The whole contents of the safe wouldn't move him to connect himself with this job."

"The job must be done by day and during office hours?"

"Yes."

"And cannot be done without the assistance of this girl?"

"You've heard."

"Very well; I have a scheme. Now listen to me."

Not even the rat which at that minute nibbled at Fellows's boot heel could have heard what followed. The panting of two breasts was, however, audible; and when, fifty minutes later, both crawled out of the cellar window among the rubbish which littered the rear of this once holy place, the one was trembling with excitement and the other with fear. They parted at the first thoroughfare, neither having eyes to see nor hearts to appreciate the touching scene which miles away was taking place in a little flat not very far from Harlem. An old man, frail in body, but with a sturdy spirit yet, was looking up from his pillow at the loving face of a young girl who was bending over him.

"I cannot sleep to-night," he said to her; "I cannot sleep; but that must not disturb you. I have so many things to think, pleasant things; but you have only cares, and must rest from them. You look very tired to-night, tired and worried. Leave me and sleep. I want to see you bright in the morning."

CHAPTER XI

The next day there was a dearth of assistants in the office. One was sick, one had pleaded a long-delayed vacation, two had business for the concern which took them into different quarters of the city, and Mr. Beers, who was next in authority to Mr. Fellows, had been summoned to serve on the grand jury. Perhaps it was this knowledge that Mr. Beers would be absent which had led to the manager's easiness in regard to the others. For he had been easy, or so Miss Lee thought when she arrived in the morning and saw the office almost empty. However, it did not trouble her much. On the contrary, the quiet and non-surveillance of the two clerks who did the business of the day seemed rather to elate her, and she went about her work, copying letters and taking down notes with an alacrity and air of cheerful hope which caused the manager to cast toward her more than one suspicious look from his desk in the adjoining room. He was not busy, though he had been the first to arrive that morning; and he had brought with him a large square package which he had taken into the room which held the safe. He pretended to be busy, but any one watching him closely would have noticed that his eyes, and not his hands, were all that were engaged, and they were anywhere but on his desk or the letter he appeared to be reading. An observer would also have noticed that his nervousness was of the extreme sort, and that the trembling which shook his whole body increased visibly whenever his glance fell on the door of Mr. Beers's private room, opening at his back. No one was supposed to be in that room to-day, and had Miss Lee not been one minute late this especial morning, perhaps there might not have been. But in that one minute's grace a man had entered the office who had not gone out again, and where could he be if not in that one closed room?

The room which held the safe was open as usual, and many of Mr. Fellows's glances traveled that way. He had entered it once only since his first hurried visit of the early morning, but only to pull down the shade over the glass in the door communicating with the outside hall. This was his usual custom, and it attracted no attention. Why shouldn't he enter it again? He thought he would. A fascination was upon him. The problem he had given Beau Johnson to solve was to receive a test this day which would make him a rich man or a felon; but before that hour why not make his own study, his own investigation? True, he had made these many times before, but not with such lights to guide him. He might learn—

But no, the very conceit was folly. He knew his own limitations, else he had not called in the services of this crook. He could learn nothing by himself, but he might look the place over and see if all was in shape for the great attempt. That was only his duty. Beau Johnson had a right to expect that of him. If the scrub woman had moved anything—

At the thought that this possibly might have happened, he jumped to his feet and hurried into the outer office; but when he turned toward the room of the safe, he met Miss Lee's eye fixed upon him with such a keen, inquiring look that he faltered in his determination, and went in another direction instead. She knew that he had no business in that room, and she also knew that he knew she knew this. Any pretense that he had would only rouse her suspicions, and these must be lulled to the point of security, or she might not enter there herself, and on her entering there everything depended. Almost immediately upon the thought he was back in his seat, and the weary moments crept on. Would she never make her accustomed visit to that room? No cablegram had come that morning, but she would find some reason for going in. Of that he had been assured by Johnson. Why, he had not been told. "She will go in," Beau Johnson had said, and Fellows believed him. He believed everything the other said, otherwise he could not have gone on with this business. But she was very long about it. Harlowe would be coming back—

CHAPTER XII

"A Block of Steel"

Ah, he had an idea! It was not his own, but for the moment he thought it was. He would leave the office himself and thus give her an opportunity to quit her work and shut herself up with the safe. But—(was his mind leaving him?) there was something to be done first. The way must be cleared for the man in hiding to enter that room before she did. How was this to be accomplished? A dozen suggestions had been given him by his confederate, but he had forgotten them all. He was in too great a whirl to think, yet he must think; some way must be found. Ah, he had it. Taking up the receiver at his side, he telephoned to a German friend to call him up in five minutes, giving him the number of the telephone in the farthest room. This he did in German, telling him it was a joke and that he was not to insist upon an answer. Then he waited. In five minutes this farther bell rang. Calling to Miss Lee, he asked her to answer for him, saying he was very busy. As she rose, he gave a preconcerted signal on the door of Mr. Beers's room. As she disappeared in the one beyond, the dapper figure of Johnson crossed the outer office and slipped into the one holding the safe. A minute later she was back reporting the message and getting instructions, but the one thing she had to fear had been done; the trap had been laid, and now for its victim!

It was not long before that victim responded to the call. On the departure of the manager from the room Grace Lee rose, and with a conscious look toward the two clerks, slipped across the floor to the open door of the safe room. Entering, she swung to the door, which closed with a snap; then, with just a moment of hesitation, in which she seemed to be trying to regain her breath, she passed quickly across to the safe and took up her stand before it. So directly and so quickly had she done this that she had not seen the slim, immovable figure drawn up against the wall at her right behind the projection of a large bookcase. Nor did any influence for good or evil cause her to turn after she had reached the safe. All her thoughts, all her hopes, all the dreams which she had cherished seemed to be concentrated in the blank, eyeless object which confronted her, impenetrable to all appearance—a block of steel without visible opening—an enigma among safes—the problem of all problems to every cracksman in town but one— which was about to be solved if one could judge from the thrill which now shook her, and in shaking her communicated the same excitement to the silent, breathless, determined man in her rear, watching her as the tiger watches the quarry, and with the same tiger spring latent in his eye. In a moment her secret would be out, and then—

CHAPTER XIII

"I Am From Headquarters"

For just a minute Grace Lee paused before the blank door of the safe, then she passed around to an unused speaking tube in the neighboring wall. Halting before it, in low but distinct tones she began to sing the famous aria from "The Magic Flute."

All agog, with eyes starting and ears alert, the man behind listened and watched. Nothing happened.

Then came a change. Gradually her voice rose, sweet and piercing, till it reached that famous F in alt so rarely attempted, so exciting to the ear when fairly taken and fairly held. Grace Lee could take it, and as it hung, sweet and deliciously thrilling in the air, Beau Johnson saw, to his amazement, though he was in a way prepared for it, the heavy safe door slip softly ajar. She had done it with her voice. How, he could only vaguely guess. He was better educated than most of his class, or he could not have understood it at all. As it was, he laid it to the vibration caused by a certain definite note acting on some delicate mechanism set in accord with that note, which mechanism starting another and a stronger one gradually led up to that which drew the bolts and set the door ajar. Whether his theory were true or not mattered little at the moment. The event for which he waited had been accomplished and accomplished before his eyes. To profit by it was his next thought, and to this end he held himself ready for the spring which had laid latent in his eyes since he first saw her advance toward the safe.

She was ignorant of his presence. This was evident from the jaunty way she turned from the tube, still singing, but in a desultory way, which showed that her thoughts were no longer on her music. But she was not so engrossed that she did not see him. The moment that her face turned his way, her eyes enlarged, her body stiffened, her whole personality took on power and purpose and she sprang more quickly than he did and shut the safe door with one quick movement of her hand that fastened it as securely as before. Then she drew herself up to meet his rush, a noble figure of resolute womanhood which any other man would have hesitated to assail. But he was proof to any appeal of this kind. She had been quicker than he who was esteemed the readiest in his class, and he owed her a grudge, if only for that. Smiling—it was a way of his when deeply moved or deeply dangerous—he accosted her with smooth and treacherous words.

"Don't scream, young lady; screaming will do you no good. Mr. Fellows has left the business to me and I am quite competent to manage it. I am from headquarters—a detective. Yesterday you aroused the manager's suspicions, and I was detailed this morning to watch you. What do you want from Mr. Stoughton's safe? An honest answer may help you. Nothing else will."

"I want—" she hesitated, eyeing him over with an insight and an undoubted air of self-command which told the hardy rascal that in this woman he was likely to meet his match. "I want some securities of Mr. Stoughton's which he has ordered me to dispose of for him. I am in his confidence, as I can prove to you if you will give me the opportunity. I have papers at home that will satisfy any one of my right to open this safe and to negotiate such papers as are designated in Mr. Stoughton's cablegrams."

"I don't doubt it." The words came easily from the mobile lips of the wily Beau Johnson. "But it was not to do Mr. Stoughton's business that you opened the safe just now. You have had no orders to-day; you had no order yesterday. Another purpose is in your mind—a personal purpose. It is this abuse of Mr. Stoughton's confidence which brings me here. You want three thousand dollars badly!"

CHAPTER XIV

"You Do Not Answer"

She recoiled. Strong as she was, she was not proof against this surprise.

"How do you know that?" she asked, her voice losing its clear tone. "I do not deny it, but how could you know what I thought to be a secret between—"

"You and your lover? Well—we—the police know many things, young lady. We have a gift. We also have a kind of foreknowledge. I could tell you something of your future if you will deign to listen to me. Your lover is an honest man. What do you suppose he will do when he hears that you have been arrested for attempted burglary on your employer's effects?"

He had been slowly advancing as he reeled off these glib sentences, but he paused as he met her smile. It was not of the same sort as his, but it was not without a certain suggestiveness which he felt it would be best for him to understand before he threw off his mask.

"I don't know what he will do," said she, meeting the false detective's eye as she laid her hand on the safe, "but I know what I shall do if you carry out the purpose you threaten. Show my papers to the police and demand evidence of my having any bad intentions in opening this safe this morning. I think you will have difficulty in producing any. I think that you will only prove yourself a fool. Are you so strong with the authorities as to brave that?"

Astonished at her insight and more than astonished at her self-control, the experienced cracksman paused, and then in tones he rarely used, remarked quietly:

"You are playing with your life, Miss Lee. I have a pistol leveled at you from my pocket, and I'm the man to fire if you give me the slightest occasion to do so. I'm Beau Johnson, miss, a detective if you please, but also a tolerably experienced cracksman, and I want a taste of those bonds."

"And Mr. Fellows?"

The words rang out clear and fearlessly.

"Oh, he? He's a muff. You needn't concern yourself about him. The matter's between us two. Three thousand dollars for you, and a little more, perhaps, for me, and I to take all the blame."

Her eye stole toward the door. No one could enter that way, she knew. Even her screams, if she survived them, might alarm, but could not bring her help for several minutes, if not longer. Yet she did not tremble; only grew a shade paler.

"You do not answer. What have you to say?"

"This." She was like marble now. "You will not kill me, because that would be virtually to kill yourself. You cannot leave this room without my help, nor fire a shot without being caught like a rat in a trap. I want three thousand dollars, and I mean to have them, but I do not see how you are going to get the few more which you promise yourself. Certainly I am not going to aid you in doing so, and you cannot open that safe. You have not the musical training."

"No." The word came like a shot, possibly in lieu of a shot, for if ever he felt murderous it was at that moment. "I have not a musical training, but that does not make me helpless. In a few moments I shall have the pleasure of hearing you test your voice again. There's the office clock ticking; count the strokes."

She stood fascinated. What did he mean by this? Involuntarily she did his bidding.

"One, two, three, four, five, six, seven, eight, nine, ten, eleven!"

"Yes," he repeated, "eleven! And at half past your old father dies."

"Dies?" Her lips did not frame the words; her eyes looked it, her whole sinking, suddenly collapsing figure gave voice to the maddening query, "Dies?"

CHAPTER XV

"Now, If Fellows Will Stay Away"

"Yes. Such is the understanding if I do not telephone my pals to hold off. He's not at home; he's with my friends. They don't care very much about old men, and if I have not a decent show of money by half-past eleven this morning the orders are to knock him on the head. It won't take a very hard knock. He was far from being in prime condition this morning."

She had shown great feeling at the beginning of this address, but at its close she drew herself up again and met him with something of her old composure.

"These are all lies," said she. "My father would never leave his house at the instigation of any gang. In the first place, he is not strong enough to attempt the stairs. You cannot deceive me in this fashion."

"He might be carried down."

"He wouldn't submit to that, nor would the other lodgers in the house allow it without an express order from me."

"They got the order; not from you, but from him. He demanded to be allowed to go. You see, Mr. Fellows sent a message that you were hurt—I will speak the whole truth, and say dying. The old man could not be held after that. He went with the messenger."

Her cheeks were now like ashes. She had gauged the man before her and felt that he was fully capable of this villainy. How great a villainy she alone knew who had the history of this old man in her heart.

"He went with the messenger," repeated Johnson, watching her face with a cruel leer. "That messenger knew where to take him. You may be sure it was to a place quite unknown to the police and to every one else but myself. Five minutes more gone, miss. In just twenty-five minutes more you will be an orphan and one impediment to your marriage will be at an end. How about the other?"

"Oh!" she wailed. "If I could really believe you!"

"I can smooth away that doubt. If you will promise not to compromise me with the clerks or any one inside there, I will allow you to telephone home and learn the truth of what I have told you. Anything further will end all business between us and wind up your father's affairs at the hour set. I can afford to humor you for ten minutes more in this nonsense."

"I will do it," she cried. "I must know what I am fighting before—" She caught herself back, but he was quite able to finish the sentence for her.

"Before you submit to the inevitable," he smiled.

Her head fell and he pointed toward the door.

"I will trust you to guard my—our interests," said he. "Open and go directly to your own telephone."

With a staggering step she obeyed. Creeping up stealthily behind her he watched her manner of opening the door and profited by the one quick glance he got of the office as she stepped through and passed hurriedly forward to her desk. There was no one within sight. Mr. Fellows had not yet returned and the clerks were too remote to notice her agitation or pay attention to her gait or the tremulousness of her tone as she called for her home number.

"Couldn't be better," thought he. "Now if Fellows will stay away long enough, I'll be able to double the boodle I've promised myself." This with a chuckle.

Meantime Miss Lee had got in her message. The answer sent her flying toward him.

"He's gone! He's gone!" she gasped. "My old, old father! Oh, you wretch! Save him and—"

"You save me first," he whispered, and was about to draw her back into the room with the safe, when the outer door opened and a stranger entered on business.

Her agony at the interruption and the few necessary words it involved caused the visitor to stare. But she was able to make herself intelligible and to turn him over to one of the clerks, after which she rejoined Johnson, closing the door quietly behind her.

His greeting was characteristic.

"You waste breath," said he, "by all this emotion. You'll need it to open the safe."

"What guarantee have I that you will keep your part of the contract?" she cried. "I sing—the door opens—you help yourself, and you go. That does not restore to me my father."

"Oh, I'll play fair. In proof of it, here's my pistol. If on our going out I do not stop with you at the telephone and let you communicate with your father and send my own message of release, then shoot me in the back. I give you leave."

Taking the pistol he held out, she cocked it, and looking into the chambers, found they were all full.

"I know how to use it," she said simply.

Admiration showed in his face. He bowed and pointed toward the tube.

"Now for the song," he cried.

CHAPTER XVI

"It Was Not Paper I Meant To Have"

With a bound she took her stand. She was white as death and greatly excited. Watching her curiously, the crafty villain noted the quick throbbing of her throat and the feverish grip on the pistol.

"Time is galloping," he remarked.

She gave a gasp, opened her lips and essayed to sing. An awful, indescribable murmur was all that could be heard. Stiffening herself, she resolutely calmed down her agitation and tried again. The result was but little better than before. Turning with a cry, she looked with horror-stricken eyes into the unmoved, slightly sardonic face of the man behind her.

"I cannot sing! You have frightened away my voice. I cannot raise that note even to save my father's life. I'm choking, choking." Then as she caught the devilish gleam lighting up his eye, she added, "You will never have those thousands! The safe is closed to us both."

He laughed, a very low, cautious laugh, but it made her eyes distend with uncertainty and dread.

"You fail to do justice to my fore-*thought," said he.

"I took this into my calculations. I know women; they can be wicked enough, but they lack coolness. Let me see now what I can do. I cannot sing, but I have a little aide de camp which can."

Walking away from her, he approached a small table on which stood an object she had never seen in that room before. It was covered with a cloth, and as he removed this cloth, she reeled with surprise; then she became still with hope and the rush of fresh and overpowering emotions.

A graphophone stood revealed, one of the finest quality. It was set to play the air so often on her lips, and in another moment that keen, high note rang through the room,—that and no more.

It answered. Slowly, softly, after one breathless moment, the door they both watched with fascinated gaze swung slowly ajar, just as they had seen it do at the beginning of this interview, and Johnson, coming forward, pulled it open with a jerk and began to fumble among the contents of the safe.

She could have killed him easily. He had forgotten—but so had she, and there was no one else by to remind her. Had there been, he would have seen a strange spectacle, for no sooner had Johnson's hand struck those shelves and minute drawers, than Grace Lee's whole attitude and expression changed. From a terrified, incapable woman, she became again her old self, strong, self-controlled, watchful. Creeping up behind him, she looked over his shoulders as he examined with his quick, experienced eye the various papers he drew out, noting his anger and growing disappointment as he found them unavailable for immediate use. Conscious of her presence, his rage grew till it shot forth in words. Not stinting oaths, he whirled on her after a moment and asked where the securities were. "You meant to have them; you know where the ready money is. Show me, show me at once or—"

Then a great anguish passed across her face, a look of farewell to hopes sweet and dearly cherished. If he saw it he did not heed. All his evil, indomitable will shone in the eye he turned up askance at her, and though she held the means of killing him in her hand, she bowed to that will, and leaning over him, she whispered in his ear:

"It was not paper I meant to have, but—but something else—I—"

She stopped, for breath was leaving her. His slim, assured hand was straying toward a certain knob hidden partly from sight, but plain to the touch if his fingers crept that way.

"Listen!" She was gasping now, but her hand laid on his shoulder emphasized her words. "There are jewels at the other end; Mrs. Stoughton's bridal jewels. They are worth thousands. I—I—meant to take those. They are in a compartment under that lower drawer. Yes, yes—there they are; take them and be gone. I—I have lost—but you will give me back my father? See! there are not many minutes left. Oh, be merciful and—"

CHAPTER XVII

"Now For My Part of the Bargain"

He was looking at the jewels, appraising them, making sure they were real and marketable. She was looking at them, too, with a wild longing and a bitter disappointment, which he, turning at that moment to mark her looks, saw and rated at its full value.

"Well, I guess they'll do," he exclaimed, pausing in his task of thrusting the gems in his pocket to hand her a bracelet ornamented with one small diamond. "But I expected more from all this fuss and feathers. Was it to guard these—"

"Yes," she murmured, thrusting the bracelet into the neck of her dress and stepping quickly back. "They are priceless to the owner. Associations you know. Mrs. Stoughton is dead—There! that will do. Now for my part of the bargain," and bethinking her at last of the pistol, she raised it and pointed it full in his face. "You will close that door now and send the telephone you promised."

He rose and banged to the door.

"All right," he cried. "You've behaved well. Now hide that pistol in your waist and we'll step into the outer office."

She did as she was bid, and in a moment more they were crossing the floor outside. As they did so, she noticed that the two clerks had been sent out to luncheon, leaving them alone with Mr. Fellows. This was not encouraging, nor did she like the click which at this moment Beau Johnson made with his tongue. It sounded like a preconcerted signal. Whether so or not, it brought Mr. Fellows from his room, and in another instant he was standing with them before the telephone. There was a clock over the safe-room door. It stood at just twenty-five minutes after eleven.

"Hurry!" she whispered as the other took up the receiver.

She did not need to say it. His own anxiety seemed to be as great as hers, but his anxiety was to be gone. The nerve which sustained him while the issue was doubtful gave some slight tokens of failing, now that his efforts had brought success and only this small obligation lay between him and the enjoyment of the booty he had won at such a risk. She was sure that his voice trembled as he uttered the familiar. "Hello!" and during the interchange of words which followed, the strain was perhaps as great on him as on her.

"Hello! how's the old man?"

She could hear the answer. It swept her fears away in a moment.

"Well, but anxious about the girl."

"She's all right, everything's all right. Take the sick man home and tell him that his daughter will be there almost as soon as he is."

"I must hear my father's voice." It was Grace who was speaking. "I will give a cry that will echo through this building if you do not put me in communication with him at once."

Her hand went out to the receiver.

The veins on Beau Johnson's forehead stood out threateningly.

"Curse you!" he muttered; but he gave the order just the same.

"Hello! Don't shut off. The girl's nervous; wants to hear her father's voice. Have him up! two words from him will answer."

"Father!"

Grace's mouth was at the phone.

No reply.

She cast one look at Johnson.

"They're getting him on his feet," he grumbled. His eye was on the door.

"Father!" she called again, her voice tremulous with doubt and anxiety.

A murmur this time, but she recognized it.

"It's he! it's he," she cried. "He's safe; he's well. Father!"

But Johnson had no time for dilly-dallying. Catching the receiver back, he took his place again at the phone and shouted a few final injunctions. Then he faced her with the question:

"Are you satisfied?" She nodded, speechless at last and almost breathless from exhaustion. He bowed and made for the door. As he opened it, Mr. Fellows slid forward and joined him. Both were leaving. He as well as Johnson. She caught the look which the manager threw her as he closed the door behind them. There was threat in that look and her heart strings tightened as she stood alone there facing her fearful duty. Mr. Fellows was a thief! The manager of this concern was even then perhaps walking off with the booty wrenched from her care by the devil's own inquisition. What should she do? Send for Philip? Yes, that was all her tortured mind could grasp. She would send for her own Philip and get his advice before she notified the police or sent the inevitable cablegram. She was too ill, too shaken to do more. Philip! Philip!

She was fainting—she felt it, and was raising her voice to call in one of the clerks, when the outer door opened and Mr. Fellows came in. She had not expected him back. She had fondly believed that he had gone with his professional comrade; and the sight of him caused her to rise again to her feet.

"You!" she murmured, facing him in dull wonder at his renewed look of threat. "I cannot stay in the same room with you. You are—"

CHAPTER XVIII

"What Have You Done Among You"

"Never mind me," came clearly and coldly from his lips. "It is of yourself you must think. Here, officer!" he cried, opening the door again and ushering in a man in plain clothes, but evidently one of the force. "This is the young lady. I accuse her of taking advantage of her power to open Mr. Stoughton's private safe to steal his jewels. Her confederate has escaped. He had a pistol and I had no means of stopping him. But she is right here and you will make no mistake in arresting her. The booty is on her, and smart as she is, she cannot deny that proof."

With a cry, Grace's hand went up to her throat.

Then she settled into her usual self once more.

The officer, eyeing her, asked what she had to say for herself.

"A great deal," was her low answer. "But I shall not say it here. If Mr. Fellows will go with me to wherever you take people suspected of what you suspect me, I can soon make plain my position. But first I should like to send for my friend, Mr. Philip Andrews. He is with the Stickney Company, and he is acquainted with my affairs and the understanding between Mr. Stoughton and myself by which I have access to that gentleman's safe and do much of his private business for him."

"That's all right. Send for Mr. Andrews if you wish, but you mustn't expect to talk to him without witnesses. Is that your coat and hat?"

"Yes."

"Well, put them on."

Mr. Fellows advanced and whispered something in the officer's ear. Immediately the suspicious look grew in his eyes, and he watched her every movement with increased care. She saw this and stepped up to him.

"I shall not deny having this piece of jewelry about my person," she said, drawing the bracelet from its hiding place. "The man whom Mr. Fellows calls my confederate gave it to me and I took it; but it will be hard for him or any one else to prove that it is a theft, harder than it will be for me to prove who is the real culprit here and the man whom you ought to arrest. Watch me, but watch him also; he is more deserving of your close attention than I am."

Her disdain, her poise, the beauty which came out on her face when she was greatly stirred, gave her a striking appearance at that moment. The officer stared, then followed her glance toward Mr. Fellows. What he saw in him made him thoughtful. Turning back to Miss Lee, he said kindly enough, "Will you let me have that bracelet?"

She passed it over and he thrust it in his pocket.

"Now," said he, "I will go first. In a few minutes follow me and go down Nassau Street. A carriage will be at the curb. Take it. As for Mr. Fellows—"

"I cannot leave till some of the clerks come in."

"We will all wait till a clerk comes."

Mr. Fellows paled.

"Here is one now."

The door opened and Philip Andrews came in.

"Oh, Philip!"

"What is this? What have you done among you?"

It was no wonder he asked. At sight of him Grace Lee had fainted.

CHAPTER XIX

"So That Was Your Motive"

Two hours later Grace was explaining herself. She was still pale, but very calm now, though a little sad. The sadness was not occasioned by any doubt she felt about her father. She had telephoned home and learned that he had arrived there and was well, and had nothing but good to say of his captors. No, there was another cause for her manifest depression, a cause not disconnected with Philip, toward whom her eyes ever and anon stole with an uneasy appeal which her mother would have been troubled to see. But it comforted Fellows, who began to regard her threats as idle in face of the evidence of her complicity as afforded by the concealed bracelet.

The officer on duty was questioning her. Had she done this and that? Yes, she had. Why? Then she told her story—the story you have already read. As she proceeded with it, every eye sparkled under the graphic tale, and the police, who had some acquaintance with Beau Johnson, recognized his hand in all that she told. One face only wore a sneer, and that was Fellows's. But no sneer could discredit a story told with such vim and straightforward earnestness. As she mentioned the emptying of the office, each person present turned and gave him a look. The manager had undertaken a piece of work too big for him. His explanations of the presence of the graphophone in this inner office were feeble and contradictory.

But he had his revenge, or thought he had, when she came to the jewels. She had pointed them out, but only to save a worse disaster. Injury to her father? "Yes, and—" She paused and her voice thrilled. "In one of the secret drawers," she continued, "there was an immense amount of currency in large denominations, the loss of which would cripple the business, if not bankrupt Mr. Stoughton. His hand was feeling its way along the face of this drawer. In another moment he would have discovered the tiny knob by the manipulation of which this drawer opens. To save the struggle which would have ensued, I directed his attention elsewhere. I don't believe I did wrong."

"But you accepted one of these articles as your share. Do you believe you did right in this?"

"Yes. I will not mention the smallness of the share, for that makes the portion saved for the owner of little account. Yet that portion is saved. I wish it had been a larger one."

"No doubt. So that was your motive—to save this souvenir for Mr. Stoughton?"

Casting a proud look at Philip, she moved a step nearer to the table on which the bracelet lay. "Will you be good enough," she asked her interrogator, "to take up that bracelet and read the initials on the inner side?"

"R. S. T.," read the official.

"Does any one here know Mrs. Stoughton's maiden name?"

Evidently not, for all remained silent.

"Does any one here know my mother's maiden name?"

Philip started.

"Yes," he cried, "I do. Her name was Rhoda Selden Titus."

"R. S. T.," smiled Grace. "This bracelet was my mother's. Mr. Stoughton allowed me to place this keepsake and some other valuables of mine in his private safe. Gentlemen, the whole of those jewels were mine—my sole and only fortune. I was keeping them for"—her eyes stole toward Philip—"for my marriage portion, the secret and great surprise I had planned for my future husband. They are worth some five thousand dollars—my mother was the daughter of a wealthy man. They would have given us a home if I could have kept them; they would also have given my husband a start in business, and this I should have preferred, but I could not let Mr. Stoughton's securities be endangered, and so they had to go. Philip, cannot you forgive me when you think that it was through my folly the secret of the safe became known?"

"I forgive you?" He could not show his feelings, but his eyes were eloquent; so were Fellows's; so were those of the various officials.

"You can prove these statements, Miss Lee?" asked one.

"Easily," she replied.

Then they turned to Fellows.

CHAPTER XX

"A Jewel of Far Greater Value"

Grace never got back her jewels. The wily Johnson was not caught, though Fellows turned state's evidence and did all he could to have the professional netted in the same manner as himself. But she did not suffer from this loss. When Mr. Stoughton learned the full particulars of this daring robbery, he made good to her the value of those jewels, and the prosperity of this young couple was secured. He was even present at the wedding. Grace wore her mother's bracelet, but on her breast was a jewel of far greater value. On its back was engraved,

To brave G. L.
From her grateful friend, T. S.

Anna Katharine Green – A Concise Bibliography

The Leavenworth Case (1878)
A Strange Disappearance (1880)
The Sword of Damocles: A Story of New York Life (1881)
The Defence of the Bride, and other Poems (1882)
X Y Z: A Detective Story (1883)
Hand and Ring (1883)
The Mill Mystery (1886)
7 to 12: A Detective Story (1887)
Risifi's Daughter, A Drama (1887)

Behind Closed Doors (1888)
Forsaken Inn (1890)
A Matter of Millions (1891)
The Old Stone House and Other Stories (1891)
Cynthia Wakeham's Money (1892)
Marked "Personal" (1893)
Miss Hurd: An Enigma (1894)
The Doctor, His Wife, and the Clock (1895)
Doctor Izard (1895)
That Affair Next Door (1897)
Lost Man's Lane: A Second Episode in the Life of Amelia Butterworth (1898)
Agatha Webb (1899)
The Circular Study (1900)
A Difficult Problem (1900)
One of my Sons (1901)
The Filigree Ball: Being a Full and True Account of the Solution of the Mystery Concerning the Jeffrey-Moore Affair (1903)
The Amethyst Box (1905)
The House in the Mist (1905)
The Millionaire Baby (1905)
The Chief Legatee' (1906)
The Woman in the Alcove (1906)
The Mayor's Wife (1907)
The House of the Whispering Pines (1910)
Three Thousand Dollars (1910)
Initials Only (1911)
Masterpieces of Mystery (1913)
Dark Hollow (1914)
The Golden Slipper, and Other Problems for Violet Strange (1915)
To the Minute; Scarlet and Black: Two Tales of Life's Perplexities (1916)
The Mystery of the Hasty Arrow (1917)
The Step on the Stair (1923)

www.ingramcontent.com/pod-product-compliance
Lightning Source LLC
Chambersburg PA
CBHW072009170626
46813CB00005B/2087